Dreams Beyond Tomorrow

June Masters Bacher

HARVEST HOUSE PUBLISHERS
Eugene, Oregon 97402

Other Books by June Masters Bacher:

Love is a Gentle Stranger
Love's Silent Song
Diary of a Loving Heart
Love Leads Home
Journey to Love
Echoes From the Past
The Heart That Lingers
Until There Was You
When Love Shines Through
With All My Heart
A Mother's Joy
Kitchen Delights
Quiet Moments for Women

Scripture quotations are from the King James Version of the Bible.

DREAMS BEYOND TOMORROW

Copyright © 1985 by Harvest House Publishers
Eugene, Oregon 97402

ISBN 0-89081-474-0

Printed in the United States of America.

To
John Leykom
for his
inspiring reminder:
"Remember the day it rained daisies!"

CONTENTS

PREFACE

Oregon is home to nearly three million people. They have built cities from the first small settlements and laid ribbons of concrete and steel where once only rutted trails served as passageways. They have established a sound educational system from the crude beginnings of a few dog-eared books brought over the Applegate Trail. Yet here progress has not taken away the sense of "old-time togetherness" seldom found elsewhere.

What holds these people together? Some say it is the flag, with its blue-and-gold beauty commemorating the entry of the thirty-third state into the Union.

But there was an Oregon before there was a flag! And those who still share their unwritten histories with new generations say that the secret lies in the "Love thy neighbor" practice begun with the arrival of the first wagon train. Once down the western slope of the Rocky Mountains, the early-day settlers were locked in by mountains.

"We were captives in a way—captives to the unchanging ways of generations past. Our parents and their parents before them brought a proud independence in the face of poverty and often ignorance. Without each other we could never have survived. And so we became as one."

Few places in America can rival the beauty of Oregon's eternal green, its carpet of wildflowers in the spring, its burnished beauty in the fall. It is a land of memories. Even the hills seem to share their recollections of the red men who paddled up and down the white-capped waters of the fertile valleys.

It is in one of these valleys, overshadowed by "Superstition Mountain," that DREAMS BEYOND TOMORROW, sequel to JOURNEY TO LOVE, unfolds.

—June Masters Bacher

Think not you can direct the course of love, for love, if it finds you worthy, directs your course.

—Kahlil Gibran

1

To Love and Ride Away

There would be a moment alone. Then he would ride one direction and she would ride the other.

Rachel stood very still, squeezing her eyes shut to hold back the tears. The long nightmare of the six-month trip over the Oregon Trail was finished. So was the happily-ever-after dream that had sustained her.

"You're sure you will be all right, Rachel? You and Star will stay with Brother Davey and Aunt Em. You'll have Moreover and Hannibal, too."

Cole had answered his own question. If she looked up, she would see concern in his gray-green eyes. Only she was not going to look. One glance and she would melt down completely...show him what a weakling she was in spite of her show of bravery ...and how much she loved him, wanted him, *needed* him...on his own terms, whatever they were. Only there were none. Men must build

9

empires. But what about the women they left behind? What about marriage?

"Rachel?"

She knew that persuasively gentle tone of voice and braced herself against it. In another moment his strong hands would reach down, cup her chin firmly between them, and turn her face upward. Then she, Rachel Buchanan Lord, would be looking into the eyes of the man who could read her soul—her husband.

Husband? Was that really the word for the person with whom she had exchanged vows of convenience six months ago and whose marriage to her was still unconsummated?

To hide her thoughts, Rachel tried to keep her face averted even after his hands touched her face. It was no use. The overpowering grip—or was it her willingness to be overpowered?—lifted her chin and locked her revealing gaze with his compelling one. And, forgetting all else, she gloried in that shared moment. Such moments were all she had, she thought sadly, as Cole's face came closer...

Yolanda, the friend who would be riding up to meet her any moment now, had written that she herself had no "formal commitment" with a young man as yet. A formal commitment was all Rachel and Colby Lord had. Each time he had left her—before their sudden "engagement," the night of their wedding, and all the nights since—there had been good reason, just as there was now. And always he had implied that, when he returned, they would begin a real marriage. But implications were not enough. And neither was the sweet memory of standing here on this very knoll, with little Star between them, and pledging to start anew on this frontier. Not when he would be leaving the very next week for Portland.

Portland. It was hard to believe he would have to ride so far and be gone so long. "Men can love and ride away," Mother had said so long ago. But was that the kind of life Rachel wanted? She and Star were his world, Cole had said—what he would live for, fight for, die for. And yet she had never seen him so excited as when the three men came riding in from the city to "discuss terms of the contract." While the other members of the wagon train set up camp and went about the business of counting their losses on the trail in an effort to see what kind of a future they could hope for, Cole and the three men kept their distance. Once Rachel had gone to the wagon they used for their caucus and asked if they would like coffee. Cole thanked her absently, not even looking up. Later she wondered if he knew she had been there. He was too engrossed in building a city on paper.

When at last they emerged and Cole told her his plans, his eyes were shining as they were shining now . . . his face so close to hers she could reach up and touch it. Scarcely aware of her movements, Rachel lifted a fragile finger to trace the dearly familiar profile.

Unexpectedly, her forefinger—once so soft with good care but now roughened from long days of driving and repeated nights of cooking over hot campfires—caught in Cole's dark sideburn.

"Your hair should be trimmed before you go—" Rachel began, and then stopped, her face flushed with embarrassment. She had sounded like a *wife*. She was not sure Cole wanted a wife. She was not sure of anything, except that her heart was missing a beat and her legs were threatening to give way beneath her—all because Cole had taken the rough forefinger in his hand and lifted it to his lips, and was now kissing it gently.

"I'm so sorry about everything, Rachel—so sorry. You shouldn't have to work like this." His voice dropped to the low, rich tone which singled her out as the most important woman in the world for a precious moment as he continued, "Your hands should be soft—and they will be. Life will be different when I return. That I pledge."

Just pledge your love, Cole. It's all I want. But aloud she said, "I knew it wouldn't be easy on the trail—or after we reached the new land. You made it all very clear. You owe me nothing, Cole."

"Owe you nothing?" Cole sounded surprised. "Look at me, Rachel—*look!*"

With no will of her own, Rachel responded to his command. Cole's party was waiting. One last look. Then the parting. . .

How beautiful he was! Rachel had thought Colby Lord to be the most handsome man in the world that day when he came to see her father, seeking (she had supposed) to purchase her youth and beauty in exchange for a fat purse to support Templeton Buchanan's imbibing. And, while she had been shamefully wrong about that—or *thought* she had—she was right about his incredible good looks. Cole's face, its deep tan emphasized by the white shirt he wore, made him into a bronze statue. Today his eyes were translucent green pools in which she could drown. But it was the strength of his jaw, set now with determination resembling a seldom anger, that held her heart captive.

Yes, he could build that city he dreamed of. He could do anything. His was the kind of broad-shouldered faith that had brought the wagon train over impossible mountain passes, across brimming rivers, through burning deserts, and into this land of promise. Rachel often wondered if God sent this chosen man a bundle of new strength each morning for him to dole out to the weary travelers as he meted out rations. It was no secret among the group which followed Cole when the wagon train split that it was he who financed the remainder of the journey. Aunt Em had gone to great ends to tell her. " 'Course he's mighty modest—sayin' it's the Lord's money, himself bein' treasurer."

The sound of hoofbeats interrupted her thoughts. "Cole!" "Rachel—" They spoke simultaneously. A brief kiss and he had ridden away.

2

Searching for Answers

"Stop crying or we'll both drown," Yolanda said.

Rachel clung to her friend but went right on weeping. It was all too much. Seeing Yolanda after all these years brought a tear of joy, followed by another and another. Now the tears of joy mingled with those of sadness and despair. Combined, they made one great tear that felt as mighty as the Columbia River on its tortuous journey to the sea. And she was drowning in that river. It was a fitting climax.

Years ago she and Yolanda, in their formative theology, would have called Colby's leaving her a judgment from on high. And maybe it was—a punishment cruel beyond belief, until one realized that, in a very real way, it was *she* who was the transgressor, not her husband. Hadn't she used him as a means of escape from an unprincipled father who held her as collateral—no matter how hard she tried to convince herself (and Colby) that he had purchased his wife as unfeelingly as he chose his oxen?

"Come on, now!" The red-haired Yolanda, her blue eyes sparkling behind some unshed tears of her own, made another effort to tease Rachel into a smile. "I'll have to find Ma if this is going to be one of those 15-handkerchief cries."

Rachel accepted the one handkerchief which the two of them were sharing, blew her nose, and pushed at a wispy curl that defied all efforts to keep itself tucked in place beneath the golden braid of hair encircling her head. But the curl bounced mischievously over her broad forehead, letting a strand stray playfully over the high planes of her cheekbones. It was no use. Her hair was unruly—like her heart.

"I'm sorry," Rachel murmured in a choked voice. "It's just the strain of it all, I guess—"

And now losing Colby again, she added in her heart.

Yolanda's laugh came then—flutelike, the way Rachel remembered. "Oh, Darling, why explain to *me*? I've been there, remember? Six months on that Applegate Trail, where death becomes more a reality than life, the gnawing hunger, the fear—"

And, most of all, the turmoil in my own heart.

But Rachel dared not give voice to the thought. She was confused and undecided about how much to reveal even to her best friend. And, unless they could shift the topic of conversation, she would be weeping again. The Lord had held her up through the long, hard journey and had sustained her when her heart was too bruised and battered to direct her ways. Now He had set her squarely on her own two feet once the party was safe in the beautiful Oregon Country. But He would not desert her, as her husband had, causing Star to ask if

Jesus went with Daddy or stayed with them...

Yolanda tugged at Rachel's sleeve. "Come on—come on! I promised Ma and Pa if they'd let me meet you alone, I'd bring you right back. We've traveled absolutely miles, following up every rumor of another wagon train's arrival, since your letter came. Oh, Rachel, I've never been so happy in my life—but wait a minute...where's the baby?"

"Baby?" Rachel repeated the word slowly, some part of her feeling that it had something to do with her. "Baby," she said again.

"*Yours*, silly! I suppose someone at your camp's looking after her. Here's Tombstone—the nag's dead on her feet, Pa says—" Yolanda stopped in midgiggle. "Oh, Rachel, what have I done? Tragedies *do* happen...is she—all right?"

The baby...the daughter about whom she had written. Rachel's head was clearing, but her voice was still weak when she said, "Oh—Estrellita, you mean?"

"You didn't tell me her name—but, yes, I guess I mean Estre—Estre-*what*?"

Rachel thought she detected a note of puzzlement in Yolanda's voice. She wasn't sure, because the other girl's back was to her as she began untying the knot in the rope tethering the old mare to the great fir tree.

"Estrellita," she murmured, her eyes traveling incredulously up, up, up to where the top of the giant evergreen seemed to brush against the very sky. Rachel felt small, lost, and insignificant. It was such a strange land—so stretched out, so uninhabited, so newly created—a regular Garden of Eden. But God intended that His Garden be shared by a man, his wife, and their offspring. And here she, Colby, and Star were widely separated—

The thought brought Rachel back to earth with

a jolt. "Estrellita means Little Star," she said, stepping into the stirrup that Yolanda made of her hands and mounting the motionless beast which the Lee family had so correctly named Tombstone. The nag, head down, gave no notice.

Rachel scooted far back on the horse's rump and extended her hand to Yolanda. Both girls smiled that they had remembered their childhood art of mounting an unsaddled animal.

Then Yolanda sobered. Her blue eyes sought Rachel's hazel ones. "Rachel," she said in her usual direct manner, "you didn't marry an Indian, did you?"

For the first time, Rachel, who was usually far more serious and introspective than Yolanda, laughed, "Whatever makes you ask that?"

Yolanda did not laugh. "It would be important for me to know. I'd have to be the voice in the wilderness, so to speak. There's a lot of trouble, Rachel, and there will be more. And a half-breed is accepted by neither white nor Indian."

Yolanda leaned down to take hold of the ends of the rope which was to serve as a rein. Her usually pink cheeks were pale.

Rachel laid a hand on Yolanda's. "But I don't understand—"

"What made me wonder? The child's name, for one thing. Then there's the case of the missing groom. I thought maybe you were looking for a way to tell me."

A deep sigh began somewhere deep inside Rachel and, gathering momentum, came out as a near-sob. "Oh, Yolanda, there *is* so much I have to tell you . . . but, no, I did not marry an Indian. I married a—"

"Man who is everything on our long list of qualifications—and then some, unless I miss my guess.

Rich as well—or is that stone a bauble?"

Rachel lifted her left hand.

"It's no bauble. The ring belonged to my husband's mother."

Rachel was saved from further conversation as Yolanda seemed to be concentrating on the frighteningly dark strip of woods they were approaching. "A footpath here somewhere," she murmured as if to reassure herself.

Rachel stiffened. "You don't mean we're going into those woods—you spoke of Indians—let's stay out in this opening where it's safe."

"The woods *are* safe—oh, here it is!" There was obvious relief in Yolanda's voice as she spotted a near-invisible trail. "Contrary to popular belief, Indians dislike thick, dark forests. Evil spirits, you know . . . not the usual story, but it's the truth. And once you're inside you'll see one of the million reasons the Oregon Country casts a spell over its inhabitants."

Rachel was still apprehensive as her friend pulled the rope to the right to guide the slow-footed Tombstone into the jungle of trees. But, once inside, she was captivated. The sky-brushing evergreens, their feet surrounded by ferns belly-deep to the old saddlehorse, seemed to huddle together as if in thought. And nature had laid a shawl of color across their shoulders where the red-gold vine maples wove in and out. The noonday sun, slanting in from the treetops, had the substance of pure molten gold. A collage of color defying description . . . twisted, turned, interwoven . . . but melancholy . . . autumn, a time for storing . . . *together*. How could she explain?

3

The Awful Truth

"Whoa back—slow it down a little, Tombstone!"
Yolanda's voice, though pitched low, caused Rachel to jump. "No Indians, you said; but aren't there wild animals?"

"Woods are full of them." Yolanda's eyes were roguish, but there was no doubt that she was telling the truth.

"Then why are you slowing this nag? If she goes much more slowly, we'll have to get off and push!"

"It's worth the risk. I'd like the truth out of you, and I guess the best way to get it is to scare it out!"

The girls allowed themselves the luxury of a companionable laugh. How good to have a friend like Yolanda—and to be reunited with her! Her friendship was one upon whose constancy Rachel could depend. Like the seasons, such a friend returned year after year—in spirit, flesh, deeds, dreams, or memories—each time bringing a new sense of wonder, discovery, and delight. Nothing could change that . . .

"How did it all happen?" Yolanda asked.

How did it all happen? Rachel kept asking herself that question. As she tried to answer it for Yolanda, a million memories floated through her mind.

No need in going back to life in the little Eastern fishing village. Yolanda had shared that segment of her life. She knew about Mother's lingering illness and that it had cost Rachel her early girlhood years. No need of speaking too much about the Boston-bred Leona Boone Buchanan's ill-fated marriage to the liquor-loving Scot who was Rachel's father. Yolanda's father, Scottish himself but somewhat less boisterous and more God-fearing, had fished with Templeton Buchanan and knew his ways. Then where to begin? With the awful truth?

It was her friend who opened the way. "You wrote that your father came back and set himself some ambitious goals as far as your choice of a husband was concerned. I'm surprised that he allowed you to make a decision on your own."

Rachel hesitated. When at length she spoke, she was sure Yolanda noticed the silence. "Cole—Colby Lord—met his only qualification."

"And what about *yours*, Rachel?"

"Oh, yes—yes, of course!"

This time she had spoken *too* quickly. Yolanda noticed that, too.

"It must have happened in a whirlwind sort of way—his courtship and the marriage. You will forgive me if I am prying—"

"You're not prying," Rachel assured her. And it was true. They were lifelong friends, accustomed to sharing their secrets, their deepest emotions, *everything* with each other. Rachel, an only child, had needed a close friend because of her lonely life.

Yolanda, one of 11 children, had needed a friend just as much—a someone who would serve as an escape from the hard work and bedlam that she, the eldest, endured.

Rachel told her then, quickly and quietly but choosing the words carefully, how she had mistaken Cole for one of the many unwelcome suitors her father had paraded before her. *And he was not one?* Oh, not at all. Yolanda exhaled as if in relief, and Rachel hurried on to explain that her husband was a successful businessman, having inherited the import-export business in which he and his father were once engaged. Yolanda was impressed, but to Rachel's surprise she did not question what such a man would have wanted of her father. So she was able to leave the embarrassing loan and her father's mortgaging of the house to Cole unexplained—as well as her flight from her enraged father, Cole's bargaining with him, and her promise to release Cole from the wedding vows that never became a marriage. A partial explanation was best . . .

How long had they been married? Six months (glibly).

"But the baby?" Yolanda's blue eyes were as round as china teacups as she turned halfway around on the horse to face Rachel. "So *that's* it?" There was no accusation in the words, just surprise.

"Oh, Yolanda, no!" Rachel felt a rush of blood stain her face. "That wasn't Cole's business with my father—or the reason we married so quickly," her words tumbled out in quick denial. "He—Cole was coming to the Oregon Country and I had to get away—oh, it's such a long story. But you must believe me," she said a little wildly. "Star isn't Cole's—she couldn't be—not when we haven't been together—"

Aghast, she stopped. The flush was gone. She was

pale, shaken, and trembling. First, she had said too little and now too much.

"You mean," Yolanda spaced each word separately, speaking as if she had never known such a condition could exist, "you mean—your marriage is *unconsummated*?"

"Right...but it isn't the way you think...."

Rachel stopped. What *did* Yolanda think? That the child belonged to another man? Or that she had refused to become as one with her husband?

The woods around them were a pageant of reds, silvers, and golds laced with evergreen, and Tombstone's slow footsteps crunched on a carpet of leaves. Hazy resin-scented smoke rose up from what must be a settlement in a valley below, heralding the early winter that chattering squirrels prophesied. There was so much to say and nobody to whom she could say it. Cole was too far away...and Yolanda was too close...she thought disjointedly.

"We're nearing home," Yolanda announced.

"And we've talked of nothing except me—"

"And your Cinderella life. You know, your story offers hope to my sometimes-bleak life—hope for a miracle—goodness rewarded—" Yolanda's voice trailed off.

Only I'm not "good" anymore, not even in the eyes of my friend. Rachel needed to correct that but found herself saying instead, "Maybe we make too much of that girlhood fantasy. Maybe it doesn't extol the virtue of goodness—the right kind of goodness, anyway. We've let Cinderella become more of an ideal in our lives than Mary, Martha, Sarah, and all the others who played such a role in Biblical history."

"She offers more hope!" Yolanda said testily. The back of her neck had grown pink, and Rachel knew she was angry.

Of course Yolanda was right. Dreams had come true for her. The "prince" had rescued her from a mundane life. But not because she was good... more because she was beautiful. Otherwise, would he have taken her away—even when she asked?

"Yolanda," Rachel said slowly as a new thought occurred, "are we talking about you or me? Have you met a prince?"

"You'll see," she said as they came to a clearing.

4

A Little Patch of Yellow

Rachel gasped with delight as Tombstone snorted,
picked up the pace, and brought her and Yolanda
into a sunlit clearing. Grass, oblivious to the season,
carpeted the wide floor of the valley—walled in by
distant snowcaps—and wandered up the slopes of
the closer hills. The design looked beautifully
familiar. Oh, yes, the quilts that Mrs. Lee taught
Mother to make years ago.

Yolanda's mother was an expert on quilts. She
knew the names of them all, and, in need of com-
panionship when her husband was at sea, enjoyed
sharing her skill. Now this valley bore a resem-
blance to the quilt that Mrs. Lee called the "Lowly
Nine-patch" because it was made up of tiny pieces
of bright calico left from her growing family's
clothes. Rachel remembered studying the pattern,
feeling that it was somehow important for her to
memorize it.

Each block, she discovered, was truly nine patches,

five of them colored print, alternated with four little
squares of color, then set together—right angles touching—on a background of white. The remembered
blocks became the fields and gardens below, their
corners touching where the long, golden windrows
of newmown hay divided the earth from the sky.

Always given to thought (more than words,
like Yolanda), Rachel saw each piece in those bygone
days as a block of time—all stitched together, generation after generation. And, now, as if by inspiration,
that is how she saw the great valley . . . each field
a cornerstone to Cole's city . . .

"Why so pensive?" Yolanda asked as they turned
a bend which Rachel was sure would bring them
to the Lee homestead.

"I was remembering your mother's quilts. Once
she gave me a little patch of yellow and said it was
her favorite because yellow's found in sunshine,
spring flowers, and warm covers when nights are
cold. I would make my own quilt someday, she
said—"

Rachel was unable to finish telling Yolanda that
she still kept that little scrap pressed in her *Poor
Richard's Almanac* and that on dark nights, when
she was lonely, looking at it brought the vision she
now saw in actuality. But this was no time to share
a dream. The army of curious Lee children was
closing in. Some shouted in glee. Others clung to the
breeches of their elders. There would be ten in all.
But there appeared to be a hundred. They raced
around so excitedly that Rachel was no more able
to count them than she could count the creatures
in an anthill.

"Mind your manners!" Yolanda admonished as she
slid off the horse and handed the frazzled rope-rein
to one of the taller boys. He blushed, took the rope,
and turned away.

"Remember Abe?" Yolanda asked. He turned back.

Rachel nodded and smiled as she accepted the large, freckled hand of the gangling boy. "You've grown," she marveled, once she was on the ground.

At her words, Abe's flush deepened. His face looked like a pickled beet, she thought with amusement. It was hard to think of the red-haired adolescent before her as being the toddling shadow forever clinging to his sister's skirts when the two girls wanted to share their girlhood secrets. Time did fly indeed . . .

Rachel realized that Yolanda was speaking. "No time to present them all. Pa will do the honors." She giggled. "Remember how he named the flock alphabetically from the Bible? We girls don't count, you know, so Ma got to name me."

In the confusion of making their way through the swarm of children, cackling chickens, and three hungry-looking hounds, Rachel had little opportunity to examine the Lee house. She knew only that it was made of rough, unpeeled logs, and—as always—she found herself wondering how a family of 13 could squeeze inside. And yet there was something homey about the place. Maybe it was the jungle of flowers surrounding it.

Judson Lee gave Rachel no more time to think. He was pumping her hand, saying she had "growed" into a "right purty young thing," shooing the chickens away, and shepherding her and his entire flock inside the combination living-dining room and kitchen.

"She's here, Wife!" He bellowed in a voice reminiscent of having to outshout the Atlantic.

His announcement brought Nola Lee from somewhere in the shadows. Rachel had never known Mrs. Lee's age. The woman had been simply

Yolanda's mother, but now she wondered how old she was. Under 40, she was certain. And the mother of 11 children! It seemed incredible that, though worn with fatigue, the angular woman's shyly intelligent face was still attractive. Her dark eyes brightened with welcome at seeing Rachel and a smile lighted up her face fleetingly. Rachel felt a lump in her throat, remembering the sight of Mrs. Lee and her mother together—two lonely women, one overburdened with children and care, the other neglected and ill. Neither life was what she wanted. Her mind clung to that little patch of yellow for her and Cole . . . their private place in the sun . . . their home.

The first thing Rachel saw on entering was Mrs. Lee's quilting frames suspended from the rough rafters. Usually she only worked in the afternoons. It was obvious that she was trying to finish something—obvious, too, that she did not wish Rachel to see it. Hurriedly she straightened one edge of the wooden frame a bit by tightening a rope. Then with a quick motion she swung the frame upward with a jerk of the pull-cord—but not before Rachel caught a glimpse of multicolored circles looped through other multicolored circles, like rainbows playing tag across a sky-blue background. The sentiment of it tugged at her heart.

"A Double Wedding Ring," Rachel breathed in awe. "Everybody should see your quilts, Mrs. Lee. You should hang them on your clothesline!"

Nola Lee leaned down to pick up a thread from the bare floor. The motion was more to hide her flush of pleasure than to tidy up, Rachel was sure.

"Enough of the world has seen it," she said meekly.

Rachel knew then that the quilt was for her and Cole. Their first wedding gift!

She felt a lump rise to her throat and a deep sense of gratitude that she was reunited with the only friends she had had time to cultivate in her early years. There was so much to say. But it would have to wait.

"Save the woman talk till me'n me boys has partook of some vittles. Dish it up, will you, Wife?"

Mrs. Lee hurried to the open fireplace, where a black dinnerpot swung from an iron rod over the low-burning flame. Yolanda followed her mother. "My job's to bake the sourdough biscuits," she said.

"Sourdough?" Rachel's question was aimed at Yolanda's back. But it was Judson Lee who answered.

"Ye'll larn, missy—beggin' your pardon, it's ma'am now, ain't it though? Ye'll larn 'bout sourdough and the other make-do's of life here on the frontier. What I would'n give fer a batch of buttermilk biscuits—not to mention pour—"

Pour. The word brought a smile of recollection. That was Mr. Lee's word for heavy cream with which he used to cover the early blueberries back home. Whipping spoiled it, he said. She wanted to tell him that he would have his buttermilk biscuits and his "pour" now that Cole had brought cattle. But the man had seated himself at the table and motioned the boys to do the same. Rachel might be "company," but it was plain to see that she was not to sit at the table with the men.

The unfairness of his and her father's ways had never ceased to ruffle her, and this was no exception. However, she was Yolanda's guest and had no wish to embarrass her. She was about to follow the other two women when Mr. Lee issued another command.

"There will be peace and quiet in this house till roll call 'n prayer!"

All heads went down. Rachel stood where she was, lowering her head obediently, but—at the risk of appearing irreverent—keeping her eyes open enough to see. Somehow she did not think the Lord would object to that.

"Abraham!" Mr. Lee's voice was anything but reverent.

"Father of the multitude," Abe answered meekly.

If I look at Yolanda, I'll laugh, Rachel thought. *"Father of the multitude" indeed . . . a better name for Judson Lee himself!*

The roll call continued around the table: "Bartholomew, *One of the Twelve* . . . Christian, *Believer* . . . David, *Beloved* . . . Ezra, *The Scribe* . . . Philip, *Lover of Horses* . . . Goliath, *Shining* . . . Hosea, *The Prophet* . . . Jeremiah, *The Priest* . . . King . . ."

"And bless the little 'un yet unborn! Amen."

Rachel's head shot up then, and her gaze locked with Yolanda's. Yolanda nodded her head, and there was a trace of sadness in her eyes. Rachel had thought it was idle boasting on the part of Judson Lee when Yolanda wrote that "Pa thinks Ma's good for one more young one. There's a bill in Congress now to give every Oregon settler a square mile of land, along with a quarter section for each child . . . we'll be rich . . ."

Yolanda brought over a mountain of biscuits—brown, golden, and fresh from the Dutch oven in a bed of coals on the hearth. The yeasty smell reminded Rachel that she had had no food, unless one could call a cup of black predawn coffee a meal. Later there would have been an around-the-campfire gathering. But she had preferred helping Cole prepare for the journey to Portland.

And now her empty stomach gnawed. What would Mr. Judson Lee say if she simply reached across and . . .

"Go ahead 'n take one—you bein' company," he said so suddenly he must have read her thoughts. Yolanda nodded. Rachel, supposing it must be an honor to be invited, took one of the hot biscuits. The man and his sons neither looked up nor invited her to sit down. Smiling inwardly, she bit experimentally into the biscuit and found it exactly what she would have expected. Yeasty. Warm. Crusty on the outside. Tender on the inside. Not at all, she suspected, unlike the heart of her blustery host.

Mrs. Lee brought in an enormous kettle of fish and replenished the platter with fluttering twiggy hands. Finished, she pushed the graying strands of her dark hair from her tired face and leaned over to check on the men's coffee cups. *Her back's like a plumb bob*, Rachel thought—*not at all crooked from leaning over quilt frames and tables to serve those she loves*. These children undoubtedly were her "accomplishment" in life—not her "burden." And still she found time to make a quilt as a wedding gift!

Mr. Lee pushed his chair back with a loud scrape. At the signal, the ten boys rose and with a muttered " 'Scuse me" hurried out the cabin door. Only then did Rachel notice that the children had been sitting on sawed-off trunks of pitch-oozing fir trees. The ruddy-skinned giant who was their father followed her gaze.

"Gonna make some benches one of these bright days—now sit a spell. You, too, Wife. And, Daughter, bring on more coffee fer th' guest. Now, tell me all the goin's-on in th' East. Be she changed much?"

Around the table, Rachel told of life in the village—including that her father had moved into the rambling old house of her childhood since the death of her mother. She talked rapidly so he would have no time for questions, carefully skirting the fact that the unscrupulous Templeton Buchanan had taken to drinking even heavier than when they were neighbors. . .that he had mortgaged the home from beneath them. . .and then devoted himself to marrying her to a man who could support his way of life. The maneuver in conversation was less in loyalty to her father than in fear that through a slip of the tongue she would reveal that Cole had held the mortgage. . .

Rachel stirred her coffee with a trembling hand, causing it to slosh over the rim and run in a little brown rivulet down the side of the heavy mug. Absently, she wiped at the spill. Would she never overcome the anxiety she suffered about her marriage? Would memory stay green forever?

Judson Lee noticed nothing amiss. "Well, one thing I be declarin'! Your ole pappy done right well by ye, he did. Easy t'see ye be jest a plain country girl—not puttin' on airs like city folks—what 'ave ye said your man's set out to do here?"

Rachel inhaled and tried a smile. "I'm a little hesitant to say, sir. While I thank you for the compliment, I gather you do not care for the city?"

"Cities be necessary. It's city *ways* that beguile. We got our problems here, we be knowin'—what with us bein' so few in number, set agin' th' British 'n Injuns alike. But we don' go 'round askin' questions. We don' steal from each other. And we know how t'be talkin' things out with our Maker without a fancy church. Wait'll ye see us on our prayer bones down by th' riverside. But city folks is different—liable t'do most anything! Hey, Girlie, what we be doin' with this kind o'talk?"

"My husband is planning to build a city—" Rachel began.

"Hereabouts?" Judson Lee's red beard was bristling. "What denomination?"

Rachel had had her speech all prepared, based on what Cole had explained to her. That is was all in the "paper stage" now. Lots of plans to be made... decisions...permits...form of government...financial backing...

But now a troubled picture of Cole formed in her churning mind. Cole, the gentle artist who "saw" a city on the canvas of his mind. Cole, whose towering soul plucked ideas, as though they were quilt scraps, from the craggy New England landscape and brought them West. Cole, who tenderly wove those ideas into soaring flights of conversation with her ...who would make those dreams come true...if only people would cooperate. He had told her he would be facing near-impossible odds in Portland. Now Rachel knew he would face them here, too.

"Denomination?" She found herself repeating blankly.

"We be 'avin more'n enough problems with th' well-meanin' but misguided missions hereabouts. Where'd ye say he be plannin' this?"

Rachel found herself explaining—while wondering about the source of her words. The tens of thousands of people who were entering the Inland Empire would need to find a place to market their wheat and other products. They couldn't very well continue selling to one another, could they? (Mr. Lee granted grudgingly that this would be impractical.) Portland was a long way to haul. (Well, yes.) Was Mr. Lee still fishing? (He *be*!) Well, then?

"Lassie, a good salesman ye be!" Judson's face lit up like a jack-o'-lantern. "Think of it, Wife—with the little 'un bringin' us in more land and me fish findin' a ready market! By jove, we do it—providin' it not be denominational!"

"Oh, Cole hopes for many churches—someday!" Rachel said, and was surprised at the fervor with which she spoke. "But," she laughed, "remember, it's all in the dream stage now. But it will happen! You'll know that when you meet my husband. The minute I laid eyes on him, I knew—"

She stopped, feeling hot color stain her cheeks. In confusion, she glanced out at the lowering sun. "I must be getting back," she murmured.

"Yep, fer shure and begorra! Best I be takin' you myself."

Rachel and Yolanda exchanged disappointed glances. But both knew that Scotch-Irish fathers were not to be crossed. Rachel thanked the women and was tying her sunbonnet when Mr. Lee made an announcement which would bring them together the following day.

"Tomorrow's preservin' day. Ye be makin' arrangements," he said to his wife and daughter. "And ye, lass, be tellin' the rest o'th' newcomers—our way o'welcome it be."

Rachel hesitated. "I don't know. Nobody has containers."

"Then they be larnin' th' art o'dryin', they be!"

At the door Rachel whispered to Yolanda that she would bring Star and an explanation tomorrow. And Yolanda whispered back that she would share her prince! A patch of yellow day.

5

If Ever You Need Me

Once again Rachel stood on the little green knoll overlooking the valley. Again she was alone, but this time by choice. Yolanda's father had been reluctant to leave her here, but she reassured him that the camp set up by the Oregon Territory's newest immigrants was only a stone's toss away. She had coveted the moment to put her thoughts in order before joining the people she had come to call family.

Talking with the Lee family, Rachel had felt an overpowering sense of animation. Briefly she had understood Cole's excitement in what was to become his lifework. But now things had spun off-center for her again. She became the same uncertain bride she had been on the long trail—wondering, in spite of Cole's gallant words, if her husband loved her . . . if she could be the right kind of wife . . . if, indeed, the three of them could face the struggle that bit by bit she realized lay ahead.

First, she must put the past behind her...

What was it that interrupted her thinking? Everything was still. Not even a breeze stirred the crown of colored leaves on the vine maples to the left. To the right a tendril of smoke rose, unbent by the wind, where the women would be kindling a fire for the evening meal. There was no sound. It was more a feeling—a feeling that she was being watched. Yolanda had said that the Indians stayed clear of the woods. Who then? Or what?

Feeling alone and uneasy, Rachel instinctively lifted her cotton skirts above the tall grass. Maybe there would be a need of a quick getaway. Then, shyly, she dropped the material and unclenched her fists. She had caught sight of "Buckeye" Jones, Cole's trusted young wagon master approaching. His eyes squinted against the sun as they searched for her. Rachel waved, feeling both a surge of relief at seeing him—tall, erect, and serious in the saddle—and a deep sense of gratitude for his warm friendship. She had come to love Buck as a brother on the long trip.

"Good timing," he said as he climbed from the saddle. "Did you have a good time?"

"Wonderful!" Rachel said. Then, as the two of them walked briskly toward the grove sheltering the camp, she told Buck about her day. Relieved of a rider, the horse trailed behind.

When the horse snorted unexpectedly, Rachel jumped. Automatically she reached out to touch Buck's sleeve.

Buck looked at her with concern and was about to speak, but Rachel silenced him with a shaking finger. She had sensed another presence, and now the horse felt it too. Some lurking danger...no, more of an evil...

Wordlessly she pointed toward the wooded area. Buck's eyes followed her finger but not in time to see the slight swaying of the tall ferns.

"What is it, Rachel?" Buck asked softly.

And for some reason that Rachel would have been unable to explain, she gave a vague answer. "Nothing," she said in a normal tone of voice. "For a moment I thought I saw something—and I wondered what kind of animal—"

Something in Buck's eyes told her he was not convinced. She was glad they were nearing camp. Any minute now Star and Moreover, her furry shadow, would come bounding to meet them. Strange that the cluster of tents in a new and untamed land was more home already than the rambling, gloom-filled house in the New England fishing village where she grew up.

"It's because of love, isn't it?"

Rachel was unaware she had spoken aloud until Buck raised an eyebrow in question. Feeling herself color, Rachel tried to explain.

"I mean it's love that makes the difference, isn't it? Without it we are paupers—"

Rachel stopped at the sight of Star's little brown legs picking their way through the goldenrod, which was as tall as the child. Buck continued the thought where Rachel had left off.

"—and *with* it we are rich indeed. Yes, it's love that determines our wealth."

Moreover, Cole's monstrous Irish wolfhound, pushed ahead of Star, as if trying to prove his worth as a guide as well as a hunter. Rachel smiled at the scene, then turned back to Buck. He was not given to idle conversation, and his words both surprised and pleased her. His kind, gentle manner would be solace to all with Cole away.

"God has been good to us," she said, glancing up to meet his eyes. And there she saw a certain look which surprised her more than his words. It was nothing she could put a label on. Maybe that was what bothered her. Troubled, she turned away. Life had hurt him, Cole had told her without further explanation. And the hurt showed in Buck's eyes. But this was different. More personal.

"Mother!"

The beautiful word was as new and thrilling to the 19-year-old Rachel as *wife*. It had all happened so fast. One day she had been nobody's. Now she belonged to this mysterious child and an equally mysterious man—both of whom she loved with all her heart. Reaching out her arms, she embraced the tiny will-o'-the-wisp creature who had appeared from out of nowhere and accepted the new life thrust upon her with more grace than Rachel herself.

"Love comes in many guises," Buck said quietly. Then he took Star's wee brown hand in his own oversized one, and the three of them continued the few paces to camp.

A frantic voice came from the direction of the wagons semicircled protectively between the temporary tents and the river. Rachel recognized the urgency in Aunt Em's voice even before she saw the tall plushiness of her gingham-clad body darting from wagon to wagon.

"Star—*Star! Es-tre-LE-ta!*"

Little Star pulled herself erect but did not move from the circle of Rachel's arms. Her great, dark eyes were solemn.

"Yes, Senora?"

Aunt Em, who had declared herself to be Rachel's surrogate mother on the trail, saw the "miracle child" as her granddaughter. Out of breath by the time she reached her adopted family, the older woman almost panted the words.

"Oh, here you are! Don't never wander away, little

darlin'!" she half-sobbed, grabbing Star from Rachel's arms. Then, as if suddenly aware that all was well, she scolded gently, "and stop callin' your Grandpa 'n me 'Snore' and 'SnorES'! We're family. Hear now?"

Rachel and Buck exchanged amused glances. Then, straightening their faces, they joined the men, women, and children swarming around the campfire—attracted, like moths, to its flame. Excitement filled the air. The men had caught rainbow trout below the rapids of the river and the women had filled their aprons with crabapples, wild grapes, and huckleberries. The children found hazelnuts.

"A real feastin' they'll be," Brother Davey announced loudly as he came to stand beside his wife. Although a head shorter than Aunt Em, the bewhiskered little man managed to look taller. "Salad greens growin' everywhere—lamb's quarters, mustard greens, 'n dill. Like th' good Lord promised, we've reached th' land flowin' with milk 'n honey. 'Course we gotta rob them bees we found. Then, bein' a truthful man like I am, I hafta admit we brung th' milk with us—" Brother Davey ran thin fingers through his sparse, gray hair. He paused, confused by his own words.

Rachel laughed. And Aunt Em scolded. "For shame, David Saul Galloway—takin' th' Lord so literal-like! What He's meanin' is a land o' fatness. Look at this supper, I dare you, and tell me He never kept His word!"

"Maybe," Rachel said thoughtfully, "*we* could be God's servants who bring the milk to the Promised Land."

She told them then about the invitation which the Lees had extended. "And they would appreciate some milk—"

The suggestion so pleased the man who had

married Rachel to Cole that he prayed even longer than usual over the food. He sprinkled the prayer with Scripture, addressing God as "Lord of the harvest," speaking of how "the ant gathereth food in harvest," and ending with a promise that God's people would "anoint them good folks tomorrow with sweet cream 'n sprinkle th' milk of human kindness all over their heads—"

"Hearts," his wife prompted in a whisper.

"Them, too! Amen."

When at last the hungry group was allowed to eat and the dishes were scrubbed, Rachel knelt to hear Star's prayers. She asked a blessing for everyone she knew, and Rachel tucked her tenderly beneath the quilt. Then she tiptoed from the tent to look up at the starry sky alone. Longing for Cole with all her heart, she felt a tear slide down her cheek. Her little patch of yellow all but faded away.

Suddenly Buck was beside her. Was she all right? Of course she was all right! *But I wanted to be alone.* Then, ashamed of her ingratitude, Rachel apologized for her sharpness.

"I didn't mean to intrude—but we're in raw country. Every community has its bad boys. If ever you need me—" Buck offered.

Rachel nodded gratefully. Suddenly she was glad he was near.

6

Yolanda's Prince

Summer had turned its face to fall. Even the commonplace things whispered in the early dawn of a fading season: spider webs, silvered by early dew, strung between bare cornstalks like laundry hung out to dry; plush mullein stalks, their shadows squatting as if to hide from the red-orange sun; gray-green tapestry of the dry moss clinging to a speckled oak; and over the eternal green of the forests the mysterious haze of Indian summer.

Wheels of the wagons (whose ribs were stripped bare of the canvas covers) rolled soundlessly over the dry pine and fir needles. The riders were as quiet as the wheels.

What must they be thinking? Last night the brave people with whom Rachel had traveled so far for so long had been overjoyed with the idea of the "preservin' day" that Yolanda's father arranged for them. This was a land of plenty. There would be no shortage of meat. But Brother

Davey thought they needed more for the coming winter.

"Too late fer puttin' a winter garden in—that is, providin' my Emmy Girl and me decide on stayin' after Cole gits back." He had yanked dangerously hard at his sparse side-whiskers. Then, when nobody responded, he picked up the conversation he seemed to be having with himself. "A body needs more'n meat fer greasin' his innards. More'n them sour-dough biscuits we been hearin' of, too. I have it on good authority that man don't live by bread alone—"

"But by the Word o' God, Davey—not yours." Aunt Em whispered the words in a low tone. Her husband heard, cleared his throat, and walked away mumbling something about finding bottles and sacks for "puttin' up ag'in the winter."

The group had agreed on an early bedtime in order to be rested for the long day ahead. No group singing or storytelling. Buck read some of David's psalms of praise and thanksgiving. Brother Davey prayed. And the men put out the fires just after dusk.

Long after Star was fast asleep, one arm reaching out to hug Moreover, who lay near the blankets on which she slept, Rachel had lain awake. The day had been emotion-packed, layered with excitement and frustration. But there was more—something very troubling, the growing conviction that she was being watched today.

And now as the group neared the Lee homestead, Rachel wondered if her anxiety had dulled the thrill of anticipation which the others felt. This must not happen. She knew and loved both groups, and it was she who must bring them together. Cole wanted his city to be the center of gravity for them all. As the kind of wife he would need, she must carry on in his absence.

So thinking, Rachel breathed a little prayer for strength, and forced a smile. "We're almost there!"

Her voice echoed hollowly against the canyon walls. The feeling of apprehension came back, and it was with relief that she saw a billow of smoke coming from the general direction of the Lee homestead.

Introductions went so well that Rachel wondered why she had been concerned. The children raced off to play, and Moreover and the pack of hounds, after stiffly sizing up one another, decided that neither was a threat to the other.

Judson Lee pumped Brother Davey's hand so hard he all but lifted the little man off the ground. " 'Bout time we had a preacher 'round here, Reverend Brother, fer baptizin' 'n marryin', lest folks be livin' in sinful ways. Be ye plannin' t'stay?"

Brother Davey, red-faced and trying to catch his breath, was saved from answering as other men joined the two. There was a lot of handshaking. Then Mr. Lee said they had best be checking on the fires and "them talkin' women!"

Rachel made sure that Aunt Em met Nola Lee. Different as the women were in appearance and personality, it was obvious that they would become good friends. There was something about them both that warmed Rachel's heart. It was as if they knew their place on earth and lived happily within the parameters as wives, mothers, and neighbors—true daughters of the Lord. Something akin to homesickness rose within Rachel with the thought, as if fingers were probing the cupboard corners of her own heart and finding it bare. Until Cole came home! Every fiber of her being was pulled backward and forward—

backward to a love denied, forward to love ful-filled.

It was then that Rachel made up her mind. "When Cole comes back, Lord," she whispered inside her heart, "there will be no more seesawing around. I *will* find a way, with Your help—even if I have to be aggressive, like Aunt Em—" Rachel smiled at the recollection of the older woman's confiding how she "jest up'n popped the question—"

Yolanda, who had been separated from Rachel by the throng, made her way forward. "That smile, as I recall, is the wrapping for a secret. So where *is* this child of mystery...who's older than her parents' marriage but not born out of wedlock... who's not your husband's, yet has no other father ...and who—my word, Rachel, I can't even say her name!"

"Explaining Estrellita, Little Star, is as bewilder-ing as dealing with her," Rachel found herself saying slowly. "The truth is, Yolanda, I don't know her background. Cole and I have accepted that probably we never will. She appeared out of nowhere—just," she smiled, "as my mystery child is doing now."

Yolanda followed Rachel's glance and gasped. Star was picking her way through the mountains of ripe fruits and vegetables. Her great, dark eyes searched the crowd. In them Rachel read a thinly veiled fear.

"Oh, she's lost—this mustn't happen again. Here we are, Darling!" Rachel called out and stooped with arms wide open to receive the small, willowy creature that God had sent her way. She wished there had been more time to prepare for this.

"Yolanda," Rachel said, her face buried in the baby-fine blackness of Star's hair, "meet my daughter."

When there was no answer, the child raised her eyes. Couldn't Yolanda see the pleading in the little face?

"Yolanda," Rachel said sharply, "your mouth is open!"

Yolanda's mouth closed with an audible click. When there were no words, the joy went out of Rachel's day. Everything—*everything*—here today depended on the moment. If Yolanda could be made to understand, she would see to it that there was acceptance for this dark-skinned child. Rachel inhaled sharply, feeling Star's baby hand grip hers with the usual surprising strength. *Speak, Yolanda, speak,* Rachel willed, *before this orphaned child returns to the vapor from which she appeared.* If that happened, even in the dark chambers of Star's mind, life here would be impossible. Cole would have to choose between his city and his family. With the thought, Rachel's old insecurities surfaced. Determinedly, she gathered Star to her and looked reassuringly into her tormented eyes. As usual, when Rachel looked at her, the child smiled.

"Isn't she special?" Rachel realized her words were a command.

"Very special," Yolanda said tentatively. "How old are you, Estre—Star?"

Star stood as tall as her height would allow. "Me llamo Estrellita," she said politely. "Mi madre—mother mine—calls me Star. Tengo—" she began, and then corrected herself again, "I have four years. Is correct, Senorita?"

"It is fine no matter *how* you say it, Little Star."

There were tears in Yolanda's voice and a song in Rachel's heart. And, *praise the Lord*, Star's smile, usually reserved for Rachel, now included Yolanda. Yolanda smiled back.

Moreover came searching for Star, and the two of them raced away happily. Rachel realized then that her chest ached from holding her breath. She exhaled gratefully.

"Thank you, Yolanda. As you see, Star is not Indian—although it troubles me that it would have made such a difference. We'll deal with that later...but for now, I'm thankful you welcomed her. She came to us so unexpectedly—probably the lone survivor of a wagon train, Cole guesses. Yolanda, it tore my heart out. She was like a wounded baby animal looking for a place to hide from life in some dark, lonely lair on the trail. And all the while holding on to that fierce Spanish pride—"

A sharp two-fingered whistle split the world in half. "Pa's signal. Guess I'll respond till I marry—"

Ever the obedient daughter, Yolanda whirled and made ready to run. But Rachel grabbed at her friend's long cotton skirt. "Wait! We're having to shift subjects too fast! Tell me—wasn't I to meet that young man of yours?"

Yolanda's face blanched of color and her eyes took on the look of fear that Rachel had seen in Star's. "Oh, Rachel," she whispered, although they were well out of earshot of the others, "please—*please*—don't mention him. He doesn't want Ma and Pa to know...and I have so much to work out..."

"But why?" Rachel asked, letting go of Yolanda's skirt.

"It's a long story," Yolanda said, not meeting Rachel's eyes. "He had a problem—and, well, wants to think it through before meeting my family. But he can't be guilty—"

Guilty? Rachel knew with a woman's intuition that her friend was in trouble. She was almost running now—more, Rachel was sure, to escape whatever was bothering her than in response to her father's signal. Lifting her own skirts above the tall grasses, Rachel hurried to match her stride. "Who?"

"His name is Julius Doogan—and you'll like my prince—"

Rachel heard no more. *Julius Doogan! The traitor on the trail!*

7

The Voice of the Lord

"Preservin' Day" was one to be remembered. The newcomers watched in fascination as the more established settlers brought out what looked like tons of fresh fruits and vegetables—foods they were so long denied on the long trek west. Children and adults alike were wide-eyed.

"Bein' so thankful 'n all, I doubt if folks minded my Davey's long-winded prayers today," Aunt Em whispered to Rachel as she hurried past with an apronful of late sweet corn.

Rachel smiled warmly. "We were all praying with him," she assured her friend.

And it was true. There was a kind of fellowship that Rachel wished with all her heart Cole could have witnessed. It made her feel less lonely to know that in some small way she had helped bring these groups together. She felt God's presence; it was as if the Lord Himself walked among them all—a feeling totally new and wonderful to her.

47

And then she heard His voice! Rachel was so startled she was unable to make out the words. But of one thing she was certain: The Lord had chosen this place for Cole's city. Yolanda knew it too, she realized, recalling one of her friend's letters after arriving in this brave new land:

> This settlement is not a place of man's creation—not even of white man's naming. It would be a beautiful townsite—a round hill some ten miles in circumference, the north side covered with fir timber, oak, hazel, and various kinds of underwood. But who could be so heartless as to hack away the haven for deer, bear, wolves, and elk? Anyway, the timber's considered worthless, with no way of hauling it away. But there will come a day...our settlement slopes to the river of life.

Rachel laid the letter aside in her mind and pondered its contents. This land was of God's creation. Surely these were His chosen people. The timber was all here, tall and untouched by human hands, waiting to be hewn into logs. Logs which would put their loving wooden arms around a man, his wife, and their children. Logs, too, to send on down the waterways to others. For a part of her husband's dream included shipping.

The old sense of adventure, so characteristic of her maternal ancestors, came back. "I hear You, Lord," she whispered. "I hear You—and I will take my rightful place beside Cole in doing Your will in this bountiful land."

The excitement within her rose to a new height. She, Rachel Buchanan Lord, had heard the voice of the Lord—and recognized it. She, like this valley, was baptized by the river of love!

8

Recognition

It was a new Rachel who suddenly became aware of her surroundings. Her heart pumped with a newfound joy. Her heels had wings. And the people around her were more than mere mortals; they were the beloved family with whom she would spend an eternity. Even her love for Cole and Star quickened—something which she would have thought impossible. The fact that she failed to understand the transformation completely did not trouble her. Revelation would unfold like Cole's city.

So thinking, the day took on a new glory. She smiled with appreciation at the scene around her. Judson Lee was calling the roll of his offspring—this time from eldest to youngest. They stood at attention as with a certain charm, humor, and grace he made the assignments. Then they would rush to do his bidding as if they had been anointed.

"Ye, Abe," he boomed, "be the official fire-wood fetcher...Bart, the stoker...Chris, water carrier..."

"Ye women," Mr. Lee said then with the same command in his voice, "will be doin' women's work, I be guessin'—bein' designated peelers and corers ...bottle-sterilizers 'n th' like—" then, whirling quickly to the guests, he smiled winningly. "Now, wee ones—ye who're company—ye be gettin' th' best." Judson licked his lips. "Hear this! Gonna be important, ye be—apple butter tasters, jelly testers, pot watchers, basket fillers—maybe even doughnut servers fer th' hungry and coffee bringers fer th' thirsty—"

There was a chorus of delighted screams. Rachel watched with amusement and joy as the younger generation rushed away to do Judson Lee's bidding. The men, she saw, needed no assignments. There were black, three-legged pots to be dragged from the smokehouse and firewood to split for kindling fires around the blanching pots. Yolanda, she noticed, seemed to be everywhere at once with her usual domestic efficiency. Yet Rachel saw that her mind was elsewhere. Repeatedly Yolanda lifted her face to the stretch of dark woods through which the settlers had traveled this morning. Was she expecting someone? Her blue eyes looked uneasy—until they would meet with Rachel's. She would smile then. But Rachel recognized a sort of pleading.

Recalling their unfinished conversation, Rachel felt a deep concern for Yolanda. Where on earth had she met Julius Doogan, the man she herself had presumed dead? She shuddered, remembering his persuading half the wagon train to leave the main trail...and then the horror of seeing the long, silent line of watchful Indians, astride horses some of the men identified as stolen, and wearing fresh human scalps dangling from their belts...

Rachel jumped when Aunt Em spoke from behind her. "Your friend's real special. Some wife she'll be makin'—her bein' unconstitutionally incapable of anything resemblin' sittin' still! Tell me, Rachel," she went on, wiping her plump red hands on her long, practical apron, "don't you think it'd be real nice if she 'n Buck got acquainted—less'n she has herself a young man?"

Rachel felt herself color guiltily. She wished very much she could confide in the wonderful friend who had become a surrogate mother to her on the trail. But not yet—not until she herself knew more, and understood. Even then, she would have to reach the decision alone—as to how much to tell Yolanda. How did one go about telling the truth in such circumstances? The man another woman loved—particularly one's best friend—had made improper advances to Rachel, the kind that made her feel unclean and ashamed of being a woman. **She shuddered.** What if Cole found out?

"You all right, Dearie? Workin' too hard, are you?" Aunt Em reached out and put her plushy arms around Rachel's thin shoulders. Rachel felt a drop of water trickle down her neck from Aunt Em's damp hands.

"Of course I'm all right!" Rachel said bravely, but her voice did not ring true in her own ears.

Aunt Em held her closer. "You're missin' Cole, that's what—an' that's a healthy sign!"

"Oh, I do love him so much," Rachel whispered. "I just pray that everything works out—I mean, for all of us—"

" 'Course it'll be workin' out! Why, you're th' only joy Cole's known in this life. And you're not always bound on confidin', but I'm thinkin' it's the same with you. Now, I best be gettin' back before that bossy Judson passes on his ways to my Davey! Where's Star?"

Rachel pointed to where the children were watching the grownups prepare fruits for drying. Either the adults were too busy to notice Star's dark coloring or it made no difference. And the children, it appeared, loved her even more because she was different. Even as she watched, one of the larger boys lifted the child and placed her in a makeshift swing. It was probably the first one she had ever been in, but she typically did not cry out even when they swung her precariously high. Proud of her, Rachel watched until she was safely down and the other children crowded around her in admiration. So much to be thankful for! So much that the day took on an aura of unreality.

The stage had been neatly set with rough benches, rawhide-bottom chairs, culinary wares, pots of water, and baskets and baskets of crimson apples, golden corn, and late-crop beans, surrounded by a curtain of wild goldenrod and Nola Lee's prize asters.

Now round and round went the knives as the spirals of peel fell from the fruit on the carefully swept ground. Later the peelings would be washed and boiled, their juice strained, sugar added, and with their natural pectin jelled into food which would have to be tasted to be believed. The nude fruits fell with a plop into a tub of slightly salted water to preserve (the older women instructed the younger ones) their snowy-flesh color. The odor, blended with the bittersweet scent of the woodsmoke, made a heady mixture.

Now and then someone would look at the sun and, seeing the gesture, all worked with renewed energy. They laughed and sang with the kind of abandon that people in this new world used as they measured their tasks and knew they were up to the job—and more. For there *was* more. Once the apples were cored, cut into doughnut shapes, and set out to dry in the autumn sun, there were the beans.

Rachel worked as she had never worked before in her life, envisioning the well-stocked pantry she would share with her husband and daughter. So caught up was she in her vision that she scarcely heard the dinnerbell.

The women brought out the food—venison roast browned and stuck with sweet myrtle, golden biscuits surrounded by pitchers of wild honey, and deep-dish apple cobblers somebody found time to make. Coffee blended with air made heavy by the scent of peeled fruit and boiling vegetables. There was too little breeze to lift the hair of the willows along the river. But nobody cared.

Brother Davey, sizing up the tables which the men had put together with rough boards set up on sawhorses and the women had covered with white cloths, said a man had to be practical. With that, he rubbed his stomach and made his prayer short.

Without invitation, the men gathered around the tables and the women began to serve their plates. Rachel bit her lip, then set to work helping Yolanda.

"Things are going to be different when you and Cole set up housekeeping—that's what you're thinking," Yolanda whispered as she passed Rachel to deliver a kettle of boiled potatoes. "No reason women shouldn't be at that table, you're thinking—"

"It's what I'm *knowing*! Things will be different with the two of us and our children."

Yolanda sighed. "That's what they all say, I guess. It's hard to imagine, but my mother was young once. I look at her now—no time to do her hair—and walking with one hip slightly to the side from carrying a baby on it—why, do you realize that all these years she's had to do everything with one hand?"

Yolanda slipped past, but not before glancing at the direction of the woods again. *It's not the babies or her mother's life*, Rachel thought. *It's indecision about her life mate.* She herself wanted to preside over her own table with the man she'd married because she was a part of the life of a man she loved and respected. Like Aunt Em said, it would work out. Cole would found his city upon a togetherness she had helped build even in his absence. She had a right to serve at his table. Hadn't the Lord spoken to her? For now she must help here. Later she and Yolanda must talk.

She remembered then that nobody had bothered to unload the butter, which would complement the sourdough biscuits the men were devouring in dangerous quantities—and the cream for Judson Lee's "pour." Hoping it was still sweet, she hurried to the back wagon in which they had hauled supplies. Indians stayed clear of the woods. Safe enough.

She was relieved to see that the wagon was beneath a large fir which offered shade from the sun. That was good. But where on earth were the containers? Probably at the very bottom of all the quilts and light wraps brought along against the early-morning chill. Rachel stood on tiptoe, then bent forward as far as possible, feeling her skirt catch on the back of the wagon and wad around her thighs. Well, nobody was near. So what of the indiscretion? She dug deeper.

A twig snapped behind her. But Rachel had no time to move before a voice spoke dangerously close.

"Well, now, if that doesn't make a pretty picture. A beautiful young lady here all alone—and obviously in need of help. But does she think it safe out here in this wild land?"

There was no mistaking the voice—or the insinuation in it. Rachel raised herself upright and yanked frantically at her skirt, catching it against the rough board and hearing it tear. Aware that it gaped open, she grabbed at the fabric and held it to her body. Then she met the eyes of Julius Doogan.

"What are you doing here?" she whispered, trying to back away, only to pin herself to the wagon.

"Enjoying myself enormously."

Julius Doogan stood so close that Rachel could see herself reflected in his heavy-lidded, colorless eyes. She tried to speak, but it was as if a circle of ice were ringing her mouth, prickling her skin, numbing her mind and body. It was another of the recurring nightmares. The hateful man would go away. Only he wouldn't, of course. Rachel realized then that she had always known that his haunting her would never be enough, that he would appear in the flesh . . . and probably destroy her. He had been following, watching, biding his time.

As she stood frozen, the former aide-de-camp reached out to finger a loose tendril of hair that had fallen over her cheek. His touch was insultingly familiar. Rachel recoiled inwardly, and yet she was unable to move. Then the fingers left her hair and slid sensuously over her arm.

Rachel pulled away but, frozen, could find no voice. *I've lived through this a million times . . . it's all a part of the terrible nightmare . . . the half-beaten enemy.*

"Don't touch me," she whispered. The words, too, were a part of the horrible dream. Always this man seemed to have sprung out of the earth, and everything about him—the heavy head of dark hair, the bony movements, and the knowing look in his pale eyes—were the same. Only today they were sharply exaggerated. He was taller than Rachel remembered. And his clothes were elegant—too elegant for a man who had broken away from the wagon train with no apparent means of support other than guiding pitifully poor immigrants.

All this Rachel saw at a glance as she took a step backward. She only half-heard some sort of comment about her being too aloof for her own safety. Her mind had now turned to Julius Doogan's relationship with Yolanda. But first there was another question she must ask—even though any conversation with this man was dangerous.

"The others—the ones you took with you? We saw signs that," her voice broke, "some of them had suffered torture at the hands of the Indians." She paused. "How did *you* survive?"

"How naive you are, my dear Rachel. I survived exactly as your righteous husband survived—"

"Leave Cole out of this."

"Gladly. Something in your manner reinforces my suspicions. You are not man and wife at all, are you, Rachel? Not in the real sense of the word."

"I owe you no explanation." Rachel pulled herself to her full height, her manner haughty. But inside there was a pounding like the surf against her eardrums. *Caution.* She must use caution.

"The others?"

Julius shrugged, and there was no sympathy in his voice when he answered as casually as if they were discussing the weather. "Who knows? They went all directions after the massacre—except the few who had sense enough to stick with their leader—"

"How many survivors were there?" Rachel whispered.

Julius dropped his head. And when she repeated the question, he answered that there was no reasoning with the fools. *Fools, Julius?* Yes, fools! His answer came in a tense, clipped voice that forbade questions. Rachel ignored the signal.

"Most of them were killed, weren't they?" Rachel felt her voice rising shrilly, giving vent to her raw, primitive grief. "*Murdered*...because of you!"

"Careful!" The word was ground out between his teeth. "You are at my mercy, you know. What would your new friends think if they knew the great Colby Lord bought and paid for his wife? And that she has been known to wander from wagon to wagon in search of the romance missing in the contract—small wonder, being married to a *eunuch*!"

A shudder of humiliation shook her body. And then her embarrassment turned to raw fury. Only dimly aware that she had moved, Rachel felt her hand strike his face.

There was a howl of rage, and suddenly Julius Doogan's hands gripped her shoulders. His fingers, like claws, tore at the soft flesh beneath the thin sleeves of her bodice.

"You will regret that to your dying day, Miss High and Mighty! You and your blood-sucking husband, who can afford to buy a wife from the money he squeezes from the unsuspecting immigrants! You and that bastard half-breed—"

His temper, when crossed, was uncontrollable, Rachel knew, recalling the hateful scene on the trail—the night when he had made unwelcome advances which she had barely been able to fight off. Now, as then, he was choking with the fury of having been scorned. Angry curses fell from his thin lips. But Rachel no longer heard his words. Her only thoughts were of survival.

"What do you want of me?" she whispered.

Did she imagine his grip relaxed? That his manner changed?

"Your respect." There was a note of cunning in his voice.

"*Respect!*" The tightening of the talon-grip alerted Rachel. She must play this game...bide her time ...effect an escape. Lowering her voice, she said, "I don't understand."

"Oh, yes, you understand all right. Now, you listen—and you listen good! I am a respectable young man, worthy of your friend's affection—"

"But that's impossible—" Rachel gasped. "I mean—"

"It's what *I* mean that counts. You keep my secret and I keep yours. It's that simple—and that complicated. I can ruin your husband and all those fancy-pants dreams of his about a city." He paused to laugh unpleasantly. "I even have allies—one being Agnes Grant—"

"Agnes Grant—she's alive?" The talebearing woman who had caused so much trouble on the trail had chosen to go with this man when Cole's wagon train split.

Rachel struggled with her thoughts. It was not that she wished the woman dead. It was that she feared her.

The sound of children's laughter broke into her fragmented thinking. "I have to go," she whispered brokenly.

Julius did not release her. "Do we have a deal?"

Something inside Rachel was dying. "Do I have a choice?" She jerked free and ran, his mocking laughter following.

Rachel never could remember what any of them said when she returned. She was only dimly aware of voices, loose phrases, and a sea of faces—all of them out of focus.

The dark interior of her mind made Buck's eyes almost black, opaque, and unfamiliar when he came to stand by her side. Yolanda had invited them all to join in the outdoor worship services Sunday, he said. Sunday? Oh, yes, Sunday would be fine, she had murmured vaguely. Then, unaware of his look of concern, Rachel moved away.

The sun dropped lower. Suddenly it was gone, leaving a strange, yellow glow. And there was yet work to do. Twilights were long in the valley, and the women still sat with lapfuls of garden-fresh beans. Mechanically, Rachel joined the group. Later—much later, it seemed to Rachel—there was a small square of lanternlight that formed a little halo of light around the heads of the children, who sat cross-legged, working hard to outsnap their parents and wondering aloud how come there was always a moon.

Sure enough, the moon was shining through the lace of the fir trees. And by its light the men squatted over a tub, leaning back and forth for handfuls of beans, swatting at the moths which ventured away from the lantern, discussing crops, the need for an outlet for their goods, dreams of a "no-denominational church," and "politicking." Once she heard Cole's name mentioned. These, then, were the new citizenry . . . people so close to life and its meaning . . . no variables . . . home was their center of gravity . . . God's people—and Cole's.

"Oh, they'll be comin' a church if we be prayin' 'n workin' as hard on th' matter as on these con-sarned beans!" Judson Lee's voice boomed.

"Amen, Brother, *amen*," Brother Davey agreed.

"So praise th' Lord 'n get snappin', Sisters!"

Languidly Rachel selected a long bean, then snipped off the tender ends of the pod. Working and watching the others' swift-fingered movements, she listened to the crackling and snapping rhythms. There were rippling sounds as the broken tubes fell into the crisping water in two's and three's and handfuls. In the dim light each member of the group appeared to be playing a complicated instrument. Now and then a cricket or a katydid joined in and the orchestra was complete. Surely these good and wonderful people were in tune with the Lord—the same Lord who had brought Cole's wagon train safely to this chosen spot. Peace came then. It was hard to stay awake. Wasn't Star weary?

But no. The child's great eyes were as wide open with wonder as they had been all day. *This patch-of-yellow day will linger with her forever*, Rachel realized. The fires gobbling up wood faster than the boys could feed them. The great wooden spoons (wired to a broom handle lest someone be burned) stirring down the apple butter till the taster declared it just right. The jelly bubbling and bouncing in rainbow colors until it "glazed a spoon." Nothing must spoil this day for the child. And nothing must spoil Cole's beautiful dream.

Rachel's mind was clearing. As repulsive as the situation was, she must find a way to deal with it. Nobody had seen her with Julius Doogan. She would have to keep his secret. A million pitfalls lay ahead. But she would have to face them one at a time.

"Lord, You are my only Confidant. I will entrust all my secrets to You—"

Rachel's inner prayer was interrupted by a question from one of the settlers. "What time is it by your watch and chain?" he asked of his host.

"It's a standing joke," Yolanda whispered, having

come from the cabin with fresh coffee and stopped beside Rachel. "Listen to Pa's answer!"

Judson Lee did not disappoint them. Snorting, he explained in his Scotch-Irish rolling-*r*'s voice that one measured a day's work by its accomplishments, not by the slant of the sun or the placement of hands on a pocket watch. Same way with the work of the Lord. One worked on and on and on . . . till they met "up Yonder" . . . and even then there'd be no time limit set on "singin' 'round the throne" and "oilin' the gates o'heaven so the latecomers can be enterin'!"

Still and all, he said, he did own the only watch with a gold chain. And (grudgingly) the work *was* finished.

Brother Davey saved his "Amen!" until then. Obviously, he'd had enough work for one day.

In the busyness of counting out containers, sacking dried foods, and loading the wagons, Rachel lost sight of Star several times. Once she saw her all alone, leaning over a sheet of paper on which she appeared to be drawing. The child was very artistic, Rachel remembered, and especially good with faces. She'd probably sketched the face of everyone in the crowd. Rachel started toward Star but was compelled to stop when one of the women, who called herself an "old-timer, havin' come here a year ago," stepped in front of her to remind her of Sunday's church services down by the riverbank. Brother Davey had agreed to preach.

Would her husband be joining them by then?

Probably not—his business would take time—

Well, if there was anything they could do . . . Rachel smiled and explained that she was staying with Aunt Em and Brother Davey . . . also that Cole had asked his wagon master to remain with the group until his return. There could be no more trains coming through before spring—

Rachel heard Star's voice then. "Moth-*er! Madre mia!*"

Its urgency startled her. It was with relief that she saw that Star was clinging to Buck's hand, tugging him along. Once they reached her, Star held out a finished picture.

"What does it mean, Rachel?" Buck's voice was low.

And then Rachel's heart grabbed with a sense of panic as she saw recognition spread across his face. "The man in the woods," Star answered for her.

9

Solidity

In the days immediately following, Rachel felt a wretchedness she had not known since escaping the wiles of her father. She was assailed by a terrible sense of bitterness at the twist of events that brought Julius Doogan back into her life. She felt trapped. Defeated. Afraid.

Wrapped in a cocoon of anguish, it was almost impossible to think. Then she would think of Cole. Her spirits would lift and she would emerge. His reassurance would make everything all right . . .

And then she would crawl back into the protective darkness of the tightly wound threads of desperation. Cole must not know. Julius Doogan had extracted her promise—a promise too hastily given. One side of her had wanted to protect Cole against the vindictive man's threats. And there was Yolanda to consider. *But the truth of the matter is, Rachel,* the other side of her said, *that it's yourself you are shielding*. And then the stab of guilt within her breast would deepen.

If only Cole were here. If only their marriage were like other people's. If only . . . *oh, dear God, help me*, she would interrupt herself in prayer.

And Rachel would set to work with renewed vigor. There were "Preservin' Day" foods to be stored, tentative living quarters to make cozier against the increasing chill of the autumn winds, and clothes to be laundered by packing water from the river and taking turns at the one cast-iron pot salvaged back when the loads became too heavy along the mountain pass. There was the day-to-day routine of cooking over the campfire and attending to Star's needs.

One of these days, Rachel knew, there must be some thought given to her education. She wondered how far it was to the nearest school. She wondered about so many things. But most of them she pondered in her heart. The others had more than their share of worries. And (with a lift of her chin), she was Cole's wife. The other women had looked to her for strength on the trail. And she would go through each day, marking its close with a little x to show that Cole was one day closer to her . . .

In work she found mindless solidity which helped to camouflage the deep despair and loneliness within her. And she praised the Lord for that. That it was contagious there could be no doubt. There was a sameness in the solidity which was forming within the group of newcomers.

Rachel had expected them to look to Brother Davey and Aunt Em for counsel. Instead, they gravitated to her. And to Buck, of course. How wise Cole was to arrange for this strong, sensitive man, so trusted and respected by all, to be with them until his return!

It was Buck who reminded Rachel about the Sunday services. She had tried to avoid him, even while longing for him to be at her side. He was someone in whom she could confide—someone who could reassure her, and wipe away her fears of Julius Doogan by confronting him openly. But therein lay the danger . . . one slip of the tongue was all it would take . . .

On Saturday she found herself looking straight into Buck's eyes. He and the other men had been inspecting an area which was freshly scarred by the removal of timber for firewood—a lovely clearing. Rachel had been wondering just where the first cabins would be built when Buck came noiselessly up behind her.

"Thinking of homesteading?" he asked lightly.

"It all depends on Cole—" Rachel hoped Buck did not notice the break in her voice before she continued, "I mean, what he finds out in Portland. I guess he'll bring the papers—"

Buck nodded. "Rachel—" he began, and then stopped. That is when she looked into his eyes. Usually so neutral in tone and expression, they were now green-spoked with emotion—an emotion Rachel found puzzling. It was at the same time personal and impersonal, nearby and caring, *faraway*, as if rooted in an otherwhereness that nobody else understood.

"Is there something wrong?" Rachel found herself asking.

Buck took her hand gently. "I was about to ask you the same question," he said simply. "You know you can count on me—"

Then, suddenly, without either of them seeming to know how it happened, his arms were about her. Lightly. Gently. Protectively. And for one moment she leaned against the security of his strength. Then she drew away.

"You will never know what a comfort you have been—"

His smile was twisted. "But you can't confide."

"Please, Buck—not now. I don't know what you're thinking, but—"

"What I think makes no difference," Buck said, and she was relieved to note that he spoke in his normal tone of voice.

"I will take you and Star to the service tomorrow—assuming that you want to go?"

"I do indeed—and thanks for reminding me. I wonder what on earth I can dig out to wear."

"It won't matter. You will look lovely in anything." Buck walked away, and there was something in the way he hunched forward, hands thrust in his pockets, that made her sad. Yolanda surely could see the difference in these two men. Any girl in her right mind would choose Buck Jones over Julius Doogan.

Sunday dawned bright and clear, rivaling spring except that the mountaintops were lost in the silver mists of autumn. It would soon be Thanksgiving, and Cole would be home!

Rachel selected the one blue-and-green percale dress and matching bonnet she had not worn, one of the remaining garments that Cole had purchased for the trip west. Remembering the "Sunday dresses" that Mother had thought so important back home, she wondered if the dress was inappropriate for the worship service. Then, remembering the pitifully faded dresses the other women wore to the Lees', she felt overdressed. But there was no time to change; Buck's eyes told her that as he helped her into the wagon. Star, who insisted upon wearing her Joseph's-coat dress, sat between them, chatting nonstop.

Long before reaching the site, the sound of voices

raised in praise reached Rachel's ears. She and Buck exchanged appreciative glances over Star's dark head. Later Rachel was to realize that such glances—even their togetherness—accounted for the mistaken identity.

Before they could alight, once Buck had halted the team, friendly settlers had gathered around to welcome them. Rachel spotted the Burnsides, Farnalls, and O'Gradys, who had stayed with Cole's wagon train when the division came. They were mingling with new friends with the kind of solidity they had formed among themselves. Watching them, Rachel was unaware that a woman she had not met before approached to stand beside her.

"Right glad to be meeting you, ma'am," she said, causing Rachel to jump. "I hadn't oughta startle you, but I wanted to be the first to greet you," the round-faced woman smiled, "having heard how pretty you are and all. Mrs. Lord, isn't it? And that must be your nice husband."

Buck saved the moment. He came to stand beside Rachel, extended his hand to the lady, and said, "I am Buck Jones, a close friend of the family. May I introduce you to Mrs. Lord, Mrs. —?"

"Landers," the woman supplied, looking flustered.

Rachel entered the small talk and watched her newest acquaintance relax at Buck's easy manner. An even greater respect rose inside her for Cole's trusted friend. And something else: a warning. She must be very careful. Mostly, she was among friends. But she must watch every appearance of evil. That trouble lay ahead there could be no doubt. At best she could only postpone it. But she must try.

With a start, Rachel realized that Mrs. Landers was speaking to her. "—so they're just tuning it up a bit. Actual service won't get underway until Judson

Lee's here. He leads the singing proper. The Galloways are here— he's going to preach. No preacher's been here since the circuit rider. Hmmm...that was early summer. Judson chased him out, saying he was just a freeloader preaching doctrine. Judson likes Bible-pounding—oh, hear Judson?"

Yes, Rachel heard Judson. She had forgotten how much Yolanda's father loved to sing—lusty, seafaring songs, gospel hymns, and, more often than not, a combination of the two. She listened now with a smile.

> Ye, the newcomers, be lank, lean, hungry, and
> tough;
> We early settlers be ruddy, ragged, and
> rough!
> The Lord sends us manna; let us be glad—
> Swappin' peas for your garments—the devil
> be had!
> Now it be the Sabbath, so let us rejoice,
> A-showin' them British why Oregon's our
> choice!

"Sing out, young'uns!" At his command the ten sons raised high voices to repeat, "Rejoice, rejoice! Oregon's our choice!"

One glance told Rachel the sad story that the lyrics of Judson Lee's song cut close to the bone of truth. There was no shelter—not even the brush arbor that the men planned to build. Worshipers were seated along the riverbanks in orderly little lines, as if the land were laid out in pews. Children sat solemnly beside their parents, obviously wearing their "company manners" as they awaited the arrival of the songleader, the visiting minister, and the newcomers, who continued to arrive.

An arbor could be built in no time at all, Rachel found herself thinking. But the other problem was something else. Most of the men were dressed in patched overalls, and the women's dresses were faded by too many boilings in the community's few iron pots.

Judson Lee strutted down the aisle left open for him.

Formidable, but as soft inside as rising bread, the ruddy-faced giant looked out over the congregation. Rachel noted that he was one of the few men wearing white shirts and that the collar, stiffly starched, appeared to be a size too small.

The sight of the white shirt took Rachel's mind back to her parting with Cole. When Cole came back—just days away now, she realized with a warm glow—everything would be different. He would find a way to meet the needs of both newcomers and old-timers. They were well on their way to becoming one, and Cole would do the rest. And, most wonderful of all, she and Cole would belong to each other forever and ever. There would be no more shadows across her heart . . .

Buried in her thoughts, Rachel did not realize that she had stopped and that the others were staring at her. To add to her sudden embarrassment, Judson Lee chose an unlikely way of welcoming her.

"We be ready to sing now—soon as ye be seated." His eyes were focused directly on her, but there was no recognition in his stern face. "Oh, Mr. Jones— and—Mrs. Lord." It was as though he had to give a little thought to the matter before he could remember her name.

Mr. Lee's exaggerated sense of importance would have amused Rachel ordinarily. But a certain look in the eyes of the women around her erased the beginnings of a smile. There was no hostility or envy. But there was more than curiosity. What she saw was a look of awe.

As she dropped onto the grass with Buck's hand

at her elbow, Rachel cast him a questioning look. He interpreted it and whispered an answer as he tried to position his long legs in a comfortable loop.

"Admiration."

"Because of Cole's name?" Rachel whispered back as she pulled the ruffles of the long, brightly printed skirt to cover her ankles.

Buck shook his head. "Your clothes," he said through the corner of his mouth. Then, putting a silencing finger to his lips, he gave her a little wink and turned full attention to Judson Lee.

Her clothes? The simple calico skirt and white muslin blouse? Then the words in the song were true—these people had an abundance of food but no clothing, not even enough to warm them against the approaching winter. There was no way for them to get their goods to market, as she had pointed out to Yolanda's father. Consequently, there was no money even if stores were close enough to purchase goods.

Rachel forced her eyes to stay put on the song leader. But her thoughts were no longer earthbound. Without moving her lips, she sent a prayer up to where, she knew, God could hear her words—even though Judson Lee tried to drown out all but his own singing!

Thank You, Father, for my husband, who held fast to his dreams—knowing that You had a plan for him. May my love be ever as unfaltering!

Judson Lee seemed oblivious to everything around him. It was almost, Rachel thought, as if the man were in a trance. His eyes fixed on a point somewhere beyond the congregation as he stood center-stage, legs apart and hands uplifted. His rich, resonant baritone compensated for the near-wooden delivery. It filled the woods and rippled with the waters, echoing and re-echoing against the canyon walls—begging all who heard to sing.

Rachel heard Yolanda's voice from somewhere near the front. Her friend sang with the same natural ease that Rachel remembered—flutelike in its beauty. Surely the voice was not lost on Buck . . . and then guiltily she realized that she was becoming as much of a matchmaker as Aunt Em. Determinedly she joined the singers in one of her favorite hymns:

> Yes, we'll gather at the river,
> The beautiful, the beautiful river;
> Gather with the saints at the river
> That flows by the throne of God.

Something stirred inside Rachel then—something pure and sweet that transcended Julius Doogan's coming into her life again. These were God's chosen people. His Spirit walked among them. God Himself was their solidity. This Cole had known all along, she realized with sudden clarity. Cole, wonderful Cole, who had risked all else in order to bring Bibles to a starving people.

10

Even If It Ain't So

Brother Davey's sermon was short. Later his wife was to comment affectionately that his departure from the usual length was due to Judson's "jest plain outtalkin' 'im." And besides, Aunt Em explained, it was nearing mealtime, and her Davey was never known to keep others waiting.

Judson proved to be quite an orator. A venerable monarch, he welcomed the newcomers to his court. They were comers-and-stayers, he could tell. Used to be so many immigrants stopped in his house asking food that he was kept poor. Finally he was compelled to choose betwixt wayfaring strangers and his own little flock. So he put up a sign saying HOTEL.

"Didn't work like it ought, ye might as well be knowin'." The big man paused, took an oversized bandana from his hip pocket, and blew his nose loudly. Then, cramming the wadded kerchief into the breast pocket of his old black coat, he continued his story.

"Th' immigrants in them days be havin' no money, so they up and quit stoppin'. Now it got downright lonesome, sure and it did. So, after talkin' th' matter over with the Lord, I took the sign down. So," Judson's chest swelled out, "ye be welcome by both me 'n th' Lord."

There was a chorus of "Amens!" before he could resume. Sorrows of new arrivals never lasted longer than the first winter, he said. Once the winter clouds broke up and the sun of spring began to shine, their spirits would rise. The voice of the turtledove would be heard throughout the land...they would all have built cabins and put in crops...they would be "old settlers" themselves...ready to receive the next immigration...ready to erect a city, they would!

Again the shouts, followed by Judson Lee's reassurance that 'twould be an orderly period in Oregon history! 'Course now, there might be a "firkin o' idle 'n lazy men arrivin' by wagon train—maybe thieves 'n gamblers."

Rachel saw some of the newcomers seated nearby cast frightened looks her direction. She forced a smile and prayed for the best. Her prayer was answered.

The giant was now jolly. Smiling reassuringly, he assured the congregation that such "trash" would find slim pickings hereabouts. Nothing much to steal in the Oregon Territory. Little to gamble for, either. Every man would work or starve. "We be havin' no time for idlers. But we be bound to help—help 'em find outbound trails or one o'them waterbugs called ships, that is!"

With much aplomb, Judson Lee introduced Brother Davey then. "We be lucky t'have th' likes o'him," he said with conviction. "Bein' a man so widely traveled, th' good Brother Galloway's sure t'be sheddin' lots o'light hereabouts."

The good Brother Galloway wasn't so sure, Rachel felt as she watched the little man make his way to stand beside Yolanda's father. As the two men shook hands and Brother Davey nervously took his place behind the makeshift pulpit, over which he could scarcely see his audience, Rachel saw Yolanda turn from the front row in which she sat. First her eyes scanned the wooded area behind the group. Then they met Rachel's in a look she recognized only too well—the look of all women in love who hope one thing and will another... *hope* to catch a glimpse of the man she adored, but *will* him to stay out of sight.

Rachel's heart went out to Yolanda. Thinking of her own insecurities, she smiled in understanding. Yolanda visibly relaxed, and the blue, blue eyes, which should have been happy and were not, thanked her. Again, Rachel wondered what on earth Julius Doogan could be doing here. This was no place, just as Judson Lee had said, for people who were out to do others in. Involuntarily Rachel found herself, like Yolanda, looking over her shoulder. To her relief, the shadowy forest stood very still. No human presence was there. But, turning back to Buck, she shuddered.

He leaned to ask if she was all right. Again, she saw the puzzled look in his eyes. But she nodded and turned her attention to Brother Davey, who was in midspeech.

"—so I've got me no text from the lids of the Good Book. But I expect th' good Lord'll be putting His words in my mouth. If He don't, I won't—won't preach, that is. Mostly, I'm a believer in visions. That's a special privilege give to old men, the Lord Hisself says—while you young men go 'bout your dreamin'! 'Course, they both take faith—these visions 'n dreams. They take faith—and you all know what faith is, brethern and sistern."

When there were no nods or hoped-for *amens*, the itinerant preacher attempted to explain. "Faith— why faith's believin' in something so strong you know it's so even if it ain't!"

There was an embarrassing silence while the mortal man helped himself to a dipper of water from the pail on the ground. "Ah, sweet water of life!" he declared triumphantly.

Then, like a breeze awakened and beginning to stir, the mortal man became spiritual. His words came tumbling out. Love, he said was what the abundant life was all about . . . love for the Maker . . . for His children. Love between man and his mate, the Maker created from man's rib. Love for all the animals over which they had dominion. Love for *life*!

Then, with eyes turned heavenward, Brother Davey seemed to be addressing his Maker directly, who had supplied the words.

"Now, let us bring nothin' but good t'these kind folks," he said. "They need clothes? We trade 'em for wheat. And we'll see to it You'll get the praise and their tithin' money. So—till Cole gets back, let us make no friendship with an angry man lest we learn his ways . . . Proverbs 22:24. I knowed You'd be speaking the words. And that's what I mean 'bout faith! You supplied 'em so fast You had me goin' there fer awhile!"

Rachel did not remember afterward if her friend ever received his *amens*. The "Jericho Singers" (as introduced by Mr. Lee) began a sort of benediction chant. She could not understand the words, if there were any, but the sounds—soaring from velvety bass to tenor, from plaintive minor to melodious major— were enough to say that the Spirit that Brother

Davey had asked for was there. Still, the explanation of faith bothered her...Yolanda's faith in
Julius? Or was it a gnawing doubt about her own
marriage?

11

Decision

Rachel was unable to sleep that night. Aunt Em would have said it was because too many helpings of chicken and dumplings "laid heavy on a body's stomach." Actually, Rachel had eaten very little of the feast spread before the congregation after the Sunday worship service.

Insomnia came from the problems Rachel saw ahead. Instead of resolving themselves, it seemed to Rachel that they were enlarging like a soap bubble blown from a spoon. Only they wouldn't let go and float away. They would grow bigger and bigger until they exploded. What then?

When she was sure Star was asleep, Rachel crawled to the front of their tent, unhooked the flap, and looked out on the moon-bathed forest. Caught in the splendor of the scene, she longed with all her heart to talk to God. There was so much she needed to thank Him for and so many things on which she needed His guidance. But the words would not come.

Rachel raised her eyes. The stars looked so close that she could touch them. How then could the earth seem suddenly so large? So lonely?

What, she asked of the stars, *if I should lose them all?* If Brother Davey's sermon was not to their liking, he and Aunt Em would be forced to move on, she knew. Buck, she supposed, would be leaving as soon as the snows melted enough in early spring to bring another wagon train through. Maybe sooner. At the thought, Rachel clutched the canvas flaps harder. She knew nothing of her husband's arrangements with Buck. Or, for that matter, with the Galloways. They might leave at any moment. What a depressing thought!

Of course, there were the Lees, lifelong friends—until now. Rachel, shifting to a more comfortable position, realized that one way or another Julius Doogan was going to make a difference in her relationship with Yolanda. She could lose her seasoned friend . . .

"And then I would be here all alone—"

Spoken aloud, the thought was so startling that Rachel sprang to her feet, her heart pounding. Had she actually given voice to such an idea? A tremor shook her body. Was she going to doubt Cole at every parting? Allow her vision to be colored gloomily forever by the memory of how they came to be married? And then she shivered again, although the night was unseasonably warm. Any mention of the past was like a wound that ached on a rainy day.

Rachel felt such a deep longing for Cole that her eyes filled up and overflowed. The words came then, somewhat as they had come to Brother Davey this morning.

"Oh, I love Cole so much, Lord—so much—so *much*! I've been deprived of love all my life . . . so little family . . . so little affection. I was starving until I found these people—Cole, Star . . . Buck . . . the Galloways . . ."

As Rachel named her beloved friends one by one, she found herself smiling as she crept back into bed beside her sleeping daughter—aware that she sounded like Star when the child began one of her endless prayers. The smile lingered and, by the time she was halfway through the Lee family, she had fallen into an uneasy sleep.

Through her misty walls of sleep, Rachel thought she heard men's voices. It was hard to be sure whether she was dreaming.

● ● ●

In the morning, in spite of her troubled night, Rachel felt better. She had always found something cleansing and therapeutic about the dawn. One could see more clearly; darkness made a person prey to human emotions. There was no reason for her to worry about Buck and the Galloways; Cole would look out after them. And what had Julius Doogan done here? Nothing but threaten. And yet . . .

It was clear what she must do.

12

Abandoned Mine

Star was content to stay with Aunt Em, who was making "coats of many colors" for some of Star's friends. The older woman was grumbling good-naturedly.

"Might as well be gettin' on with my needle—my Davey havin' got carried away 'n promisin' clothes in exchange for winter eatin' 'n plantin'. Did you know, Rachel, these women ain't in possession of needles—let alone cloth for makin' clothes to keep 'em warm?"

Rachel did not know. But, being in a hurry to get to the Lees for a much-needed talk with Yolanda, she did not question the statement. "We'll need their help—"

She leaned to kiss Star, who was working on pictures of the dresses her other friends would like. They showed such promise that Rachel paused a moment and asked Aunt Em to look. Star, obviously pleased, favored them with a shy, sweet smile.

"See these too, please."

Star placed several pictures in Emmaline Galloway's hand. "Faces," she said simply.

"Well, I do declare! Have you seen these, Rachel?"

In a hurry to be off, Rachel glanced at the drawings quickly as they were handed to her one by one. Brother Davey, for sure. And Aunt Em. Then there was a sketch of a woman with a wealth of dark hair piled on top of her head and a hauntingly beautiful face. Something about it looked vaguely familiar, and Rachel would want to look at it again.

"My word! *Rachel*!" Aunt Em's voice was trembling—as was her hand as she gave Rachel the remaining sketch.

Julius Doogan. Rachel felt her face go white. Her tongue clove to the roof of her mouth as she saw Aunt Em drop on her knees beside Star and put her arms around the child.

"Who are they, Darlin'? Tell Grandma Em."

Star pulled away and her little face took on the look of a frightened animal again. "Faces, Senora—Grandma mine. One is a beautiful queen, yes? And the man in the woods *es muy mal*. Ask Moreover. He speaks Spanish!"

To Rachel's relief, a roguish look came to Star's great, dark eyes, changing her into a little pixie. Rachel shook her head at Aunt Em, and the nod the other woman returned was one of understanding . . .although she did not understand at all. . .

Getting away from the Lee family was easier. "The menfolk are getting the winter wood," Yolanda's mother smiled. "You girls need to talk. The little ones and I'll work on the quilt. Take along a snack. Air's bracing."

"I hope Hannibal's surefooted," Yolanda said once they were turning away from the cabin. "We'll be climbing."

"Where are we heading?" Rachel asked, seeing that they had taken a new direction.

"You'll see."

Rachel had intended plunging into the conversation immediately. Find out what she could about her friend's relationship with Julius Doogan. Do what she could to discourage it. Subtly bring Buck's name in, making mention of his possessing all the desired characteristics that she and Yolanda sought in a husband. . . finding a way to avoid disaster without telling all.

But the scenery was becoming awesome—mountains stretching as far as the eye could see, gorges, ravines, and silver waterfalls. The mountain air was exhilarating. Rachel felt herself drifting into an exalted state, making it almost impossible to keep her mind on the task at hand. If only she could wish away today and dream of her tomorrows. . .

Rachel's thinking was cut short by Yolanda's reining in ahead. The path had become so narrow that they must ride single file, and Tombstone had obviously been this way before.

Up, up, up they traveled. At length Yolanda stopped.

At Yolanda's signal, Rachel dismounted. The horses were standing against a near-barren mountain—beautiful in its starkness because of the white glittering of the soil in the sunshine. The scene should have been peaceful, but Rachel was unable to shake off a sense of uneasiness.

Yolanda, on the other hand, seemed perfectly at ease. "I love it here—and aren't you hungry?"

Without waiting for an answer Yolanda took a jar of coffee from a cloth sack. It would be cold but wet, she explained with a smile. Rachel nodded and tried to concentrate on how to open the conversation that they must have.

Yolanda was either totally unsuspecting or choosing to avoid it as long as possible. She kept up a flow of small talk. Ma had sent along generous wedges of dried prune pie. She did hope her mother left the seed in like always. Did Rachel remember when as giggling girls they had counted the seed of Ma's cherry pies to learn their fate?

Yes, Rachel remembered but gave no voice to the frightening outcome the counting always brought. "Rich man, poor man, beggar man, *thief*; doctor, lawyer, Indian chief . . ." If neither girl liked her fate, she would take another bite and start anew on the list of men she might or might not marry. Invariably, it was Rachel's good fortune that she was to wed a rich man; poor Yolanda's to marry a thief.

"It was just a game," Rachel said. "Surely you've outgrown being superstitious."

Yolanda handed her a wedge of pie before answering. "I guess I have," she said slowly, biting into her pie before continuing. "I'm *sure* I have—or I wouldn't be *here*! This is Superstition Mountain, you know."

Rachel felt a tingle along her spine. But before she could ask questions, Yolanda had leaned down to pluck a dried daisy from the shining soil.

"He loves me, he don't; he'll marry, he won't! He would if he could; but he can't—"

"Go on," Rachel said, taking a prune pit from between her teeth. "This one's new to me. I'm amused."

"I'm not!" Yolanda spoke the words harshly. Then, regaining control, she said, "It's not amusing to run out of petals—"

"What would the next petal have foretold, Yolanda?"

"I thought you didn't believe this stuff." Yolanda

busied herself wiping her hands on her handkerchief.

"I don't. I just want to know the next line."

Yolanda sighed deeply. "He won't," she all but
whispered. Then, brightening, "But we know
better."

Yes, they knew better. But Rachel also knew that
something was troubling Yolanda—troubling her
deeply.

"Let's jolt that down with a little walk," Yolanda
said. "Then we'll talk."

She tied the sack to Tombstone's reins and tethered both horses. Then she pointed to a little path
that led still higher, perhaps to the peak of the
mountain.

The granite was slippery. Watching their footing,
the girls were unable to talk until, breathless, they
neared the summit.

"This is as far as we go. It could be dangerous,
Julius says—"

"*Julius?*" Rachel had overemphasized the word
before she was able to stop herself.

Yolanda gave no indication of noticing. "Legend
has it that fire was handed down from heaven on
top of this mountain. You know the Indians—most
superstitious people on earth, apart from our Irish
ancestors! Their lives are hazard-filled and, being
unlearned, they look for answers in nature. Good
and evil supposedly had a battle over the keeper of
that flame...oh, well, that gives you some background. It'll serve to show why we don't want Pa
knowing where we've been today—else there'll be
fire flying at home."

Rachel's head jerked alert. "What are you saying?"

"Simply that, being of Scotch-Irish blood, he listens
to some of this foolishness. It's good in a way, as now
this has become the private meeting place of my

prince with me. Someday," she said dreamily, "we're going to build ourselves a castle up here. . . surround it by the lochs that Pa talks about when he's homesick. . . plant it with heather. . . and hide it with Scottish mists. There'll be no road up, of course—just one that leads down," she giggled, "in case we run out of ambrosia—"

Rachel tried to smile through stiff lips. "When does all this take place?"

"You don't believe me, do you? It's not just the dreaming. You don't believe any of it."

"I didn't say that."

"I could hear it in your voice, Rachel. All right, we know each other too well to play games. It will take place as soon as the man I'm going to marry is free. He's too noble to ask me to share his life until the ridiculous charges are cleared."

"What charges, Yolanda?"

Yolanda held her finger out to a butterfly. "You'd think this little creature would have given up." Moving her finger upward, she watched in fascination as the butterfly whose wings were battered by the summer's flight came to rest on her fingertip. Then she resumed talking almost to herself.

"He brought part of an ill-fated wagon train to safety when the other leader would have taken their money and their goods. Don't look so shocked, Rachel. There are people like that."

Yes, Yolanda, there are. But it's the other way around. . .

Rachel longed to cry out. To protest. To set things straight. This might be her only chance. But she could only nod woodenly and listen as if she were in a stupor as Yolanda talked on. When Yolanda sat down, she sat beside her.

There was an Indian attack. Julius Doogan was the hero. . . putting the needs of the others before his own...binding up wounds (he knew a lot about the anatomy, really should have been a doctor, you know). Of course, food gave out (the unprincipled leader before him having taken all the supplies). That's why he did what he did.

What did he do, Yolanda? Rachel must have asked the question she heard the other girl answering.

People were starving. Men, having lost their strength, were unable to work. Babies were dying. There wasn't time for the delays involved in home-steading. So he borrowed money—only the men he dealt with did not call it borrowing. They accused him of *stealing* when he took in a bag of what looked like gold nuggets but actually was "fool's gold."

"There, I've told you the truth. And you don't believe it—so surely you'll see why I know the others won't either!" Yolanda looked at Rachel defensively.

Rachel's initial shock was wearing off. She felt a mounting fury at the nerve of this man. Correction: One could hardly call Julius Doogan a *man*! He was a beast.

Swallowing hard to control her rage, she spoke as normally as possible. "But the man you speak of—wouldn't they have checked on the story, taken the rocks to an assayer?"

Yolanda's voice was defensive when she answered. "He *had* one gold nugget—lent to him from one of the immigrants."

"How many immigrants have you known in possession of gold nuggets, Yolanda?"

Yolanda leaped to her feet. Rachel reached a hand up for help in the little game they had always played. Yolanda did not take it. Instead, she took a few steep steps upward. Then, pausing, she looked down at Rachel.

"There is an abandoned mine at the top—caved

in once, and countless men were buried alive. That's one reason the Indians fear it . . . ghosts, you know . . . but Julius just wants nothing happening to *me*—oh, Rachel, what's the use? There can be no peace between us until we resolve everything. You'll feel differently when you meet him—"

I have met him, Yolanda. Rachel longed to blurt out but did not dare. Getting slowly to her feet, she kept her face averted. Yolanda would guess she was holding something back at one glance.

"There's nothing wrong between us, Yolanda, that love can't fix. It's just because I care so much about your happiness . . . and it all sounds so—so frightening."

"I'm not frightened!"

"Maybe you should be. Or, if not frightened, at least cautious. What do you know of this man really?"

"What did you know of Cole?"

Rachel felt a tightening around her heart. "We aren't talking about my marriage right now. But, believe me, I can respect the man I married. I added that to our list, Yolanda—put it close to the top, in fact. Do you respect this man?"

Yolanda, Rachel saw from the corner of her eye, was twisting her skirt with nervous hands. The butterfly had flown from her finger and was circling her head. When in exhaustion it tried to light on her shoulder, Yolanda brushed it away. "Go die," she said harshly. "Your cycle's finished."

Somewhere inside Rachel an alarm sounded. Maybe this thing had progressed farther than she had imagined. Her head cautioned her to leave it alone. But her heart advised something far different. Driven by a force beyond her control, Rachel raised her eyes to meet Yolanda's stormy ones.

"Have you prayed about this?"

"You know I have!"

The tears in Yolanda's voice twisted Rachel's heart but did not deter her. "Together?"

Yolanda dropped her eyes to her pointed shoes and stood immobile for what seemed an eternity. When she spoke, her words were filled with anguish.

"Rachel, *please*," she whispered, "please let's not talk about it anymore. To put it simply, I would rather be unhappy with Julius than happy with somebody else. Does that make sense?"

It didn't. But Rachel knew that Yolanda had been pushed as far as she dared push—for now. And she, too, felt drained.

Forcing a smile, she said, "Well, so much for the Cinderella myth. Rags to riches, Prince Charmings who ride white horses and sweep us away to their castles—all that's all right, maybe, as long as we don't internalize it too much. I never did like the part where there was only one 'good' girl, while the ugly stepsisters stirred up conflict. Life's not like that. That writer never knew about us pioneer women— women getting along with other women—in the reality of it all—"

"Making quilts, drying fruit, and tossing babies in the air?" Yolanda was trying to smile.

"Exactly. And *praying* together! Now, will you take my hand?"

After the prayers, the girls hugged each other. Rachel was not sure anything was settled, but she felt lighter of heart. Their problems were in God's hands, and something told Rachel that this was the first time Yolanda had surrendered the matter to Him.

They rode in silence for a time. The path, sloping steeply downward, was uneven. Granite in the sparkling soil was slippery and there were stones underfoot. The horses had to pick their way carefully. Yolanda rode ahead, and Rachel saw her take her eyes from the narrow trail several times to search the dark stretches of woods. It occurred to her then that Julius Doogan must live—hide out, actually—in the vicinity of Superstition Mountain. It was isolated, but she wondered if there could be another purpose. If so, what could it be?

Caught in her thoughts, Rachel was never sure how it happened. Hannibal seemed to stumble over a stone and she was thrown from his back without warning. She cried out as the ground rushed up to meet her. And then all was dark.

From another world she heard a girl's voice screaming, "Julius—help, *help*, HELP!" Then someone was leaning over her—someone who smelled of leather and horseflesh. Someone who was calling her name. It was not Cole—or Buck—but he was saying she would be all right while the girl (Yolanda?) was asking over and over, "But how did you know her name?"

13

Back from the Dead

Rachel, wondering how to explain her bruises, limped into camp. Immediately she realized that in the commotion no explanations would be required.

People appeared to be milling everywhere. The whole world seemed to have tilted. No longer did the blue-ribbon day seem idyllic; the water, crystalline; and the surroundings, serene. Now when she had so coveted peace and quiet, there was bedlam.

Rachel, trying to push her way through the crowd, was intercepted by Brother Davey. "What happened?" she begged.

The little man held onto his gallus as if it were a weapon. Almost jumping up and down in frustration, he held out a scrawny arm. "See here? See what she's done, my Emmy Gal? Sewed a button on my shirt-sleeve, she did—"

"Calm down, Brother Davey, and tell me the problem."

"The problem is that now I can't blow my nose without scratchin' it!"

In the face of impending disaster, the comedy of the well-meaning man's ways went unnoticed. Rachel's eyes were searching for Buck, who could bring some kind of order.

But it was Aunt Em who rushed away from Liz Farnall and Mandy Burnside to join her. Opal Sanders, holding the twins, and Elsa O'Grady, who sat nursing the new baby—an expression of desperation on her face—looked to Rachel as if for direction. Their needs loomed more important than the problem.

I must help them. But how? My strength must be their strength until Cole comes back. Until Cole comes back?

Weak-kneed and dizzy from the recent fall, Rachel wondered if she had struck her head...if today's confusion were really happening...if she had seen Julius Doogan...if (she thought a little wildly) she had a husband at all...

"You all right, Dearie?" Aunt Em's arms were comfortingly around her. "That man!" Her head tipped to the right, where her husband stood speechless. "David Saul Galloway's about as helpful as a tree-bound squirrel in a crisis. Who cares 'bout buttons when human life's at stake?"

Releasing Rachel, she said, "We got trouble, Rachel—real trouble. It's gonna take prayerful thinkin'."

" 'N prayerful *doin'* as well!" Her husband was suddenly alert, appearing to have had the "words put in his mouth," as he had received them on Sunday. " 'Him that's got two shirts—' " Brother Davey paused to look down at the niggling button, " 'let 'im share with 'im that ain't got none'!"

"*Coats*, Davey," Aunt Em corrected absently.

"Luke 3:11, remember? '. . . and he that hath meat, let him do likewise.' "

"But they got no meat. They got nothin' to offer but trouble—and we've arranged th' swappin' o'shirts—coats if you'd rather—fer food with old-timers. So I vote—"

Rachel put a restraining hand on Uncle Davey's arm when he would have lifted it as if in announcement of having reached a decision on his own. "Please," she said softly, although her heart was beating uncomfortably fast, "won't *somebody* tell me what's going on?"

The Galloways talked at once then. It was hard for Rachel to make sense of what they were saying in their excitement. But she heard enough—enough to know that Aunt Em was right. There was trouble—real trouble.

The survivors of the wagon train had "returned from the dead," both declared. Rachel remembered, didn't she—them what followed that no-good Doogan when he caused division, claiming it was because the plodding of the cattle was slowing the train. . . snow would fall. . . all would perish?. . . *Yes, yes. . . Rachel remembered.* Well, they all but starved, they did—them what escaped the massacre—and now Rachel should *see* them. . .

As the story unfolded, Rachel did see them in her heart. The desperate eyes in faces like skulls. The ribs pressing against the children too weak to move. The distended bellies. . .

"They're here?" Rachel whispered incredulously.

"Here 'n beggin'—" Brother Davey began.

"Not beggin', Davey," Aunt Em said softly; "askin' alms—not far removed from what our own plight was when Cole took us in."

Not far at all, Rachel's heart cried out. Aloud, she

asked where the survivors of the "Cowless Column" were.

"Best I take you," Brother Davey said. "Buck's speakin' with 'em in the grove."

Rachel walked the few paces to where the women in Cole's group seemed to be waiting for her. "It will be all right," she promised, wondering if it would. "I'll go help—"

It seemed fitting that the sky had gone suddenly dark. A sharp east wind whipped at the vine maples, scattering their leaves over the hills like flame. The fir trees bent and sighed, giving with the wind of the storm, just as Rachel knew she would be called upon to do. *Stay close, Lord,* she implored.

Brother Davey, more in control of himself, led her toward the grove. There he paused to call over his shoulder, "Hustle some grub, Emmy Gal. Them folks is hungry!"

The rest was like a dream. Mercifully, Rachel's eyes refused to focus on the pathos before her. Her legs, still trembling from the fall, threatened to give way. Surely her body would have floated into space had not Buck come to stand beside her. With his supporting hand on her elbow, somehow she stood before the group—nothing functioning except her ears.

Too spent to speak with passion, the newest immigrants told their piteous story. The massacre took over half the train, even children caught playing along the river. One woman told of seeing men lying face-upward on the rocks by the river who, having lost their wives and children, were careless of the rain falling in their faces. They no longer willed to live. Women offered their last decent clothes for a few potatoes to keep themselves and their children alive. Rain turned to snow, causing them to lose their way. The rough and desolate country into which they wandered was without game and without potable water. Stock got out of control...nearly everyone became ill from dysentery...strong men wept.

What became of their leader?

Julius Doogan had to strike out ahead to keep from being killed by angry people. Had to keep away from the immigrants to save his life from men whose wives had been tortured and killed by Indians...even hid out among a tribe of Indians himself, so they thought.

Thought? Was it otherwise?

"He was held hostage—as if we could pay—but we was wrong 'bout his character. He sent word of a waterin' hole—even sent some supplies by a scout—"

"And a message tellin' how to find you—and help."

Rachel's eyes sought Buck's. For a moment his face swam crazily before her eyes. And then her vision cleared. *There are loopholes in the story*, his eyes signaled. But Rachel turned away, ashamed that she dare not nod.

The story became more bizarre. Having exchanged their clothes for food, some perished from cold when snow caught them before they could find a pass leading to the south side of Mount Hood. The cattle trail which the dwindling number found was too narrow for wagons. So they took the straw from the mattresses and fed it to the horses. The women and children were put on horseback...men tried to take a shortcut—an old missionary trail...a few broke through and managed to get to this settlement...starving, homeless, pleading...

The dreadful story ended. There was silence. And then a question split the tomblike quiet.

"Where's Doogan?" Rachel had never heard Buck's voice so harsh.

"He's lookin' out fer us—like your leader is. Up in some big city—Portland, ain't it? He'll be stakin' claims. . ." The answer came quickly, almost accusingly.

Rachel did not need to look up. She would know the voice of Agnes Grant anywhere. Even in her greatest hour of need, the woman's voice was sharply honed with defensiveness.

Finally it was over. Rachel stumbled away, dimly aware that Buck still supported her with strong hands.

"I'm going to be sick," she gasped. "Oh, Buck, where was God?"

"Easy, Rachel," he said softly. "Milton would have asked, 'Where was *man*?' "

14

Decision Without a Choice

Rachel was attempting to explain to Star what had happened when Buck shook the flap of the tent. She welcomed his presence and hurried to let him in.

"But tell me the rest of the story, Mother mine," the child implored, her great, dark eyes looking up at Rachel. "Are we not the Good Samaritans, yes?"

Rachel was appreciative when Buck scooped Star up and soothed her. In a language the child would understand, he explained that it must be a group decision. Therefore, the ending of the story must wait until after tonight's meeting.

"The people are being fed now—"

"Loaves and fishes?" Star was enjoying the drama.

"More likely beans and biscuits, Darling," Buck laughed. "Now, if you will let me put you down, I will tell Mother about tonight's meeting—after she explains those bruises she's wearing!"

The statement came suddenly. And, feeling overwhelmed by the torment of the past few weeks,

Rachel found herself pouring out the account of the afternoon, omitting only the presence she had known was there when she fell.

Buck's expression was grim as he watched her fumble with the folds of her skirt. Finally he spoke.

"You haven't told me the whole story, have you?"

The spark of hope that he would notice nothing amiss was quickly extinguished. Rachel felt herself color guiltily. She despised deception—and especially over a man not worth his salt!

"I don't know what you mean," she said, disliking herself tremendously for being coy with so straightforward a man.

Buck sighed deeply. "Oh, Rachel," he began. Then, seeming to change his mind, he said, "Has nobody cautioned you about the dangers of the mine?"

"You mean about all the ghosts and goblins?" Rachel tried to tease lightly.

But Buck's voice was serious, his face grave. "I mean the cave-in at the mine, the inactive volcano—and other things. Yolanda's father warned me that the ground could crumble. . .and surely Yolanda has told you what she told me."

For a single moment, Rachel forgot decisions that must be made this fateful night. In the forefront of her mind was the news that Yolanda and Buck had talked. How much. . .?

But her thinking was cut short by a question which she later realized she may have misread. It came too unexpectedly.

"Was *he* there, Rachel?"

Again, the sick yearning to confide in Buck, to be rid of this guilty conscience mingled with fear and shame that twisted and turned inside her, begging for release.

She opened her mouth, then closed it. With a suffocating sensation tightening her throat, she could only whisper, "I can't tell you more...I am bound by promise..."

There was hurt in Buck's voice. "I understand—at least, I am trying to. The man is why your friend does not wish to become better acquainted with other men, isn't he? But why am I asking when you have promised?" Determinedly, he squared his shoulders and his voice took on the strength so characteristic of him when he spoke again.

"Why then are we talking of inconsequential things? I want you to come with me to the meeting tonight, Rachel. The decisions reached will be critical to your future with Cole."

"And yours, Buck. Cole will want you to stay, and I—we need you, even Yolanda, although she may not have realized it yet."

Something of the old hurt came back to his face. "We shall see," he answered with no inflection in his voice.

Buck became the businessman then—kind but brisk. The men of the groups would caucus again ...try to crowd into one of the tents if it rained... make an attempt at working out some kind of arrangement whereby all could survive. It did not occur to Rachel to suggest that perhaps her presence would be peculiar in the masculine group. Cole had discussed the plans for the needed city so often with her that she could see the layout in her mind. And then there was the secret she held in her heart—memory of the Voice which gave her no choice but to serve where she was needed.

The meeting went well. And yet throughout Rachel felt uneasy. At first it was something she was unable to put her finger on. Then gradually the uneasiness shaped into objects that were clearly visible in her mind's eye.

Julius Doogan! Where was he? Supposedly in

Portland. But he could be lurking in the shadows. How like him to have thrust these people upon her conscience, using them as a shield of protection! She might do her duty as she saw it and reveal his presence. But she would not turn these people away. Well, on that her conscience was clear. These people played no part in her decision . . .

And, still, there was Agnes Grant! There had been no sign of repentance in the meddlesome woman. How many had she influenced? How many were enemies here? How many were friends?

Rachel stilled her thoughts then in order to listen to Buck. He welcomed the newcomers and spoke of the American drama which had preceded their arrival. The old-timers of several years hence had come in "peak years" from every state and country, driven by oppression, poverty, and in many cases the law. They had heard that the Oregon Territory promised streets of gold. Instead they had found hardship—hunger, disease, often death. True, Oregon was the land of promise. But it took time for land to be cleared and seed sown—and the eventual harvest. And, Buck explained, even when the fields were white with harvest, there was the grave question of where and how to dispose of the goods. Hence the need for the city.

"We need you just as you need us. Here there is a grave need for all of us to put to work Paul's teachings. I beg of you all, believers and nonbelievers, to hear this message."

Without waiting for a signal of approval, Buck reached for a Bible. Rachel noted that the Book opened without the aid of a bookmark.

> For as the body is one, and hath many members, and all the members of that one body, being many, are one body, so also is Christ. . . .
> And whether one member suffer, all the

> members suffer with it . . . . And God hath set
> some in the church . . . apostles . . . prophets . . .
> teachers. . . . Covet earnestly the best gifts:
> and yet I show unto you a more excellent way.

"Somehow," Buck said soberly as he closed his Bible, "we will survive. But there *must* be cooperation. There must be trust. There is a need for organization—a form of government, if you will. And there is a need for rules, respect for the rights of others . . ."

Buck hesitated. Then, looking at the silent group, he said with conviction: "I personally feel that all rules should come from the Bible. And, thanks to a wonderful man who felt that the soul needed nourishing as well as the body, we have enough copies so that all who wish will have enough to read."

From somewhere in the crowd there came a muffled "Amen," echoed by a chorus which rose in volume. Buck had done a commendable job of attempting to draw the factions together. Except for the gnawing awareness of Julius Doogan and what might be his planted spies, Rachel could almost believe that the division on the trail had never happened.

But it *had* happened! Rachel realized with sudden clarity that she had been thinking only of how the sudden appearance of these people would affect her directly. Now she stole a glance around her. And everywhere she saw the same doubts, the same fears, the same suspicions.

These, the troubled faces said, *are the half-beaten enemy—those who took our horses, slaughtered our cows, stole our supplies, betrayed our leader. . . and among them may be the men who would have defiled our women. . .*

The silence was filled with remembered anguish

of those wronged. Rachel remembered, too. But, looking at the wasted faces of those who had wronged their fellowman, her heart was filled with compassion. Their loved ones were hungry. For them, they would come crawling into what could be an enemy camp. What would Cole have her do? The answer was clear. Her husband would have her do as the Lord willed: Forgive as He forgave.

Rachel rose to her feet. In a calm voice which she hardly recognized as her own, she said quietly, "We are called upon to forgive."

The silence thickened. It was as if the men's breath was caught in their lungs, rendering them speechless.

Then there was a sudden angry shout. "Forgive!" Rachel recognized the voice of Liz Farnall's husband. "How many times?" His voice tapered off wearily.

Rachel raised her eyes to meet Buck's. "Seventy times seven?" Buck nodded.

Brother Davey, having kept quiet as long as possible, hurried forward to stand beside Buck. Dwarfed by Buck's giant height, the little man stood on tiptoe, bristling. "Less'n you return to your folly like'n a dog to its vomit!"

Quotation of the proverb broke the tension. There was a snicker followed by a whisper, which gave way to a confusion of voices. Rachel felt her spirits rise for the first time. Talk—even heated talk—was better than silence, she thought as she sat down quietly. Closing her eyes, she turned a smile toward heaven. God would handle the rest.

Minutes later there was a unanimous vote from the "Cow Column" (as Buck still differentiated those who had followed Cole from the newcomers) to accept the "Cowless Column" by acclamation. The loud round of applause was no surprise to Rachel— and she was sure no surprise to the Lord either!

Rachel slipped unnoticed from the tent and hurried to tell the good news to the waiting women. Accustomed to waiting, they had sat quietly—praying, Rachel suspected, and keeping the coffee hot until their men returned.

At her news, one by one those who had journeyed with Cole came to hold her close. Rachel could feel the hard beating of their hearts and taste the salt of their tears. And then the women from the other column came shyly forward, their eyes begging forgiveness and understanding. Their waiting had been the hardest of all. Rachel reached out to the gaunt body closest to her. It was easy to understand the torture of waiting—having waited so achingly long herself...

"Good news, Dearie!" Aunt Em was saying as she blew her nose. "Now, somehow, we're all a-gonna pitch in here and make things work till our leader gets back..."

She went on then to tell of how they themselves had been befriended by the earlier settlers. "So, you see, one good deed deserves another. That ain't Bible, but it's the gospel truth."

Little Star, wearing the long nightie that Aunt Em had made from an old blanket, came from the tent to hold Rachel's hand. "Verdad!"

Rachel smiled at the beautiful child. "Yes, truth."

But from the shadows came the unmistakable voice of Agnes Grant. "You had no choice!" she mumbled.

15

Meeting at the Mine

The day before Thanksgiving was somber, bleak, and cold. One of the men brought wild turkeys into camp and Aunt Em scalded the birds in preparation for plucking away the pinfeathers. Abe, Bart, and Chris—the three eldest sons of Judson Lee—came to extend an invitation from their parents to bring their "offerings" and join them and their far-apart neighbors for prayer service and dinner the next day. Buck rode back with the boys to explain the presence of the newcomers. The hospitable Lees sent a message that they were to be included by all means. So there was a great deal of rejoicing—but none in Rachel's heart. She felt lonely, depressed, and unaccountably restless.

Feeling the need to get away, she tied a scarf around her head and—leaving a wide-eyed Star to watch Aunt Em prepare the turkeys—saddled Hannibal and rode away in the mists. It was good to be alone. Good, somehow, to feel swallowed up in a misty silence where there was no need for conversation, no need for glossing over situations which she knew were potentially dangerous. Good to have no problems to resolve. She was a girl again. A girl very much in love—in love with the most wonderful man in the world. And yet, she realized as she let the stallion pick his own path, it was becoming increasingly hard to remember Cole's face.

Oh, Cole, her heart cried out, *don't stay away too long. . . lest we lose what we have. . .*

In an effort to squelch the little voice inside her which mocked, *What do you have, Rachel?* she loosened her grip on the reins and gave Hannibal his nose. As the horse galloped along, Rachel suddenly became aware of the direction he had taken. The abandoned mine loomed in the distance. Wrapped in fog, it looked even more eerie than before.

Here alone in the half-light, it was easy to understand the superstitions of the Indians and the somewhat cautious approach of the settlers. The sound of the wind whistling over the ashen peak seemed to carry a warning: She should turn back. And, yet, she was unable to issue a turning command to Hannibal. It seemed imperative to continue to the forbidden territory, either to prove to herself that no departed spirits inhabited the place or, more likely, to try to discover for herself what the mine's secret could be. Somehow it seemed to hold the key to a certain strangeness which prevailed here.

At first she had found perfect peace here among the settlers in the wild and beautiful country. The trees moved back to provide wide horizons and yet closed in protectively. The river sang incessantly. And flowers sprang eternal. "Peaceful Valley" would have been a good name, she thought, as Hannibal—panting—reached the shelf near the summit. Only the peace she sought upon leaving her conniving father was not here—not peace in its perfection.

Dismounting, she pursued the thought. Fear blocked the way to peace, she decided. There seemed to be a constant fear in the hearts of everybody she met . . . fear of poverty . . . fear of war. Rachel frowned as she tethered the horse, remembering fragments of conversations among the men which they seemed to assume the women could not understand. Possible war with Great Britain. Possible war with Russia over territorial rights. And inevitable war with the Indians.

But the real war she herself fought was within herself. There was the niggling fear that sooner or later Julius Doogan must be faced and the growing fear that although she too was emerging into a leader unexpectedly, she and Cole—her very life— might be growing in opposite directions.

Hannibal snorted, causing Rachel to jump. But the sound brought her back to the present. Just what she expected to find, she was uncertain. She only knew that she must climb the remaining steps to the top of Superstition Mountain.

How desolate and grim it looked! How different it would look if there were men working the mine. She wondered for the first time if it had been abandoned.

Near the mine shaft, Rachel picked up a stone and examined it. It had no sheen. Because there was no sun? Or because it was worthless? Probably the latter, she supposed, tossing it into the gaping mouth of the ancient volcano. When there was no sound to reassure her that it reached the bottom, Rachel found herself shuddering. What had possessed her to come here, anyway?

She was about to turn and hurry back to where

Hannibal was tethered when she heard the stallion give a peculiar neigh. It was as if the animal, too, were bewitched by the strange surroundings and had become a creature of the wild.

She took one backward step and lost her footing on the slippery granite soil. For one terrifying moment, her body swayed precariously on the rim of the black pit. In that twinkle-of-an-eye suspension between life and death, Rachel knew the truth. It was evil men, not evil spirits, one need fear here. Though the why of it she might never know . . .

When two strong hands gripped her arms, Rachel made no protest. It was preordained . . . a "judgment from on High," as she and Yolanda had thought of punishment so many years ago. *I do not deserve to live. I do not have the courage to stand even after God has spoken . . . go ahead . . . push me into the bottomless pit . . .*

"Why are you here? *Why?* Don't move . . . "

The whisper could belong to anybody. Rachel, her back still to the speaker, stood rigid, waiting, her eyes closed. Julius. It had to be Julius. But when the viselike grip relaxed and she felt herself being pulled gently backward, she knew it must be Buck. Her relief was so great that she wrenched herself free to reach grateful arms to him.

"Buck—oh, Buck—I should have known you would come," she sobbed, burying her face in the warmth of a woolen jacket without looking up.

Later Rachel wondered how long the two of them stood wrapped in the misty silence, broken only by her diminishing sobs, before she realized something was wrong. There should be words to reassure her, make her feel safe. Instead, there was a strained silence.

She must release herself. But she found herself not

wanting to struggle. Something inside her wanted this. It belonged in the recurring dream in which she lived with Cole, loved him, spent the rest of her natural life as his wife...

Cole! The words brought her to her senses.

"Let go of me!" she cried, more angry at herself than at the man who held her.

"Oh Rachel—Rachel, my darling—" There was anguish and heartbreak in the low, rich voice she would know anywhere in the world. *Cole!* Her head spun dizzily. *How...where...why?* Wretchedly, she knew that she had hurt him deeply.

16

Lost Moment

Rachel had dreamed of the reunion over and over. Always she would be beautiful. Her hair would glisten from a rainwater shampoo. She would smell of lavender. And she would be wearing flowers in her hair. Best of all, there would be the kind of understanding between her and Cole that required no words—the language that only lovers knew.

As it was, her hair, wet by the thickening fog, clung dankly to her face, and Brother Davey's oversized jacket that Aunt Em had insisted on throwing around her shoulders undoubtedly smelled of wet wool. And how could there be understanding when she had called her husband by another man's name? *Now* where was all the aggression of Aunt Em's that she had planned to use? Rachel felt tears of despair mingling with the damp of the fog as Cole led her carefully down the slippery path. If only Cole would say something!

At the ledge where the horses waited, Cole

stopped. She heard him inhale deeply as if about to speak, but no words came.

It was Rachel who took a step forward. "Cole—up there—I want to explain—I—"

"Never mind back there—except that I don't want you near the mine anymore. It isn't safe. There are things you do not know—"

Things she did not know. That was the third warning Rachel had received, each from a different man. "I don't understand, Cole. I went there because I was afraid—"

Rachel's voice trailed off. She had not known how to complete the thought. Cole did not pick up the conversation immediately. Neither did he move to untie the horses.

Instead, he took the small step remaining between them and caught her in his arms, kissing her gently at first and then almost fiercely. "Oh, Rachel, if anything should happen to you, I couldn't bear it. You are my reason for going on. I held you like this as I sat through the long meetings with men who don't understand dreams! There were times when I thought you were the only one who believed in me. And one was enough, because it is all for you!"

"And yet it is holding us apart." Rachel was surprised at the edge of bitterness she heard in her own voice.

Cole's arms tightened around her. "Not forever, my darling—"

All the frustration and uncertainty, the waiting and longing buried inside while trying to give more strength to the other women than she herself possessed, were suddenly too much. Tears blinded her eyes. She gulped hard, then yielded to the compulsive sobs that shook her body. "What proof do I have that things will ever be any better?" she cried out, aware that her wail was that of a disappointed child.

But Cole did not treat her like a child. "You know it is true," he said simply, "because you know that I love you—have always loved you from the moment you greeted me so graciously as the unwelcome suitor—"

Rachel blushed. Aware that Cole had released her and, holding her hands, was leading her to a rock pile, she offered no resistance. Now spent, she felt small, shaken, and foolish.

"Not much of a loveseat," he grinned. Pulling a blanket from the back of his horse, Cole spread it over the damp boulder.

"Sit down," he invited. When she did not respond, he said gently, "There is no need to be afraid of me—"

"It's not you I'm afraid of, Cole," Rachel said carefully. "It's us—"

Cole drew her down beside him gently but persuasively. Then, unbuttoning his heavy mackinaw, he pulled her head and shoulders inside against the warmth of his chest. Through the heavy wool shirt, she could hear the heavy rhythm of his heart.

"*Of* us or *for* us, Rachel?"

Rachel felt a wonderful drowsiness stealing over her body. How could she be so excited by his presence and so completely contented at the same time? The answer did not matter. Nothing mattered. This moment alone with Cole was the healing balm she had so needed. It dispensed with all her wretchedness, doubts, and fears. She was more certain than ever before that, no matter what dreams this man must follow, all she wanted was to be with him always and forever. . .

"I am not afraid anymore," she whispered from

the dark intimacy against his chest. " 'There is no fear in love.' "

"First John 4:18," Cole said without hesitation. "John's writings are among my favorites. 'Love is of God,' for instance. I think He meant that in every sense of the word."

Yes, there was indeed a holiness about a love such as theirs. Rachel raised her head and kissed his cheek. She felt the day's heavy growth prickle her face. He must have ridden all night. How selfish she had been.

"Oh, my darling, you must be worn out—"

"Not so worn out that I am willing to leave here letting you believe I am content with a Platonic marriage, my love." Cole kissed her gently. He threw off her wet scarf and ran his hands through her sodden hair. "I love you."

"In such a setting?" The little laugh died in her throat. The setting was her husband's arms—no matter where. And this was where she belonged, in a dream wider awake than she had ever been before in her life. Breathless with wonder, yet sharply and ecstatically conscious of his lips on her forehead—his arms holding her tenderly but breathlessly close. Nobody had ever felt like this before. Nobody ever would again. The moment belonged to them. And in her delirious joy of loving and being loved, Rachel felt a sort of sadness that the rest of the world would never, ever know the mad-sweet wonder of floating with them into the clouds—and on into heaven . . .

And then the spell was broken! There was the startling sound of a horse's hooves nearby, followed by an uneasy whinny from Hannibal.

Rachel raised her head from Cole's chest and followed his eyes as they searched the trail below. He did not speak but held her hand so tightly that she could feel the blood throbbing at the end of her fingertips.

Then, appearing like a phantom in the fog at first, a horse and rider took shape. The rider apparently was unaware of their presence. He stopped and appeared to listen.

Was it her imagination or did he wear a dark cape? Surely the strange Indian legends and Scotch-Irish ghost stories could be only dark imaginings. All the same, a lump of fear rose in Rachel's throat. She looked to Cole, hoping his expression would set her mind at rest. But his face was flushed with anger. When she turned, the rider had disappeared.

"That is why I do not want you here. We must go!"

But *why*? There was no time for talk. And the lovely moment was lost. Her heart searched for answers that her lips dared not seek.

17

Choosing of the Council

It seemed fitting that the mist should turn to heavy rain, making further conversation impossible. Cole helped Rachel mount the stallion and wrapped Brother Davey's coat around her. He remounted and they rode single-file down the mountain. As they entered the meadow, he pulled alongside her and cupped his hands to his mouth.

"There are men with me," he shouted above the wind. The rest of what he said was drowned out by the rain. Rachel caught only fragments: "...meeting tonight...need for immediate shelter...to Portland again...so sorry...but dare not risk delay..."

Nothing delayed except their togetherness. And Cole was sorry. Did he have nothing more to say? Gone was the mountaintop elation. Up there she had believed that her husband loved her as she loved him—with the kind of love that could not be denied. But now he was telling her that their love must be cast aside. Rachel wondered then if happiness was not for pioneer women at all. . .

Nobody in camp had seen them approach. Visibility was near zero in the blinding rain. Rachel could see the sodden tents, so reminiscent of the trying days on the long trail to Oregon, and knew that others' needs must be put before her own in spite of her heartache. But how? And how long?

Cole made it easier then. There, with the rain beating against their faces, he helped her dismount. Then he gathered her to him for a long-to-be-remembered moment of tenderness.

In the kind of whisper that was almost a groan he said, "If I could remain here with you I would be happy, no matter what my lot, just because of you, my darling Rachel. When we are together the whole world seems kinder, more gentle and loving. I am alive as never before. Do you believe that?"

Wordlessly she nodded. Then there was bedlam. They were surrounded by a throng. Star was screaming, "Dad-*dee*, Dad-*dee*, Daddy mine!" over and over while trying to have him all to herself by binding his legs together with her fragile brown arms. Aunt Em was hovering over Rachel, scolding, then tugging her away for dry clothes and broth. Faces blurred together, including the face of Agnes Grant. It was then that Rachel remembered there had been no opportunity to tell Cole about the reappearance of the errant group. She wanted to ask Aunt Em if perhaps the decision to bring these people back into the group was premature—maybe unwise—when it was Cole to whom they must look for financing during the first winter. But the older woman was spooning broth into her mouth. And she was too weak to push it away. It was easier to swallow than resist, Rachel remembered thinking, and then she drifted off to sleep.

The smell of coffee awakened her. At first the surroundings looked unfamiliar. Slowly the clouds of sleep receded and she recognized the Galloways' few belongings.

Cole! And Star! Where were they? She tried to raise herself on an elbow, only to be pushed down gently by the capable hands she had come to depend on.

"Drink your coffee before tryin' t'put some sanity to th' day," Aunt Em advised. "You slept th' night through like a newborn—didn't even rally when Cole stripped them wet garments off—"

"Cole *what*?" She was wide awake then.

Aunt Em nodded. "And be careful with that cup, Dearie, less'n you spill coffee on that robe. Mighty sweet—matchin' the pink in your cheeks 'n all."

For the first time, Rachel looked at what she was wearing. The beauty of the gray flannel wrapper, piped in pink sateen, caused her to gasp in admiration. "Cole brought me this—and he—he—"

Aunt Em busied herself with a tray she had brought in, purposely avoiding Rachel's eyes. "And jest you wait'll you see what else. Bolts o' calico . . . needles . . . seed—"

"But there can be no planting until we know about the homesteading."

"Oh, Cole has all th' proper papers—even th' men fer fixin' 'em up. Real gentlemen, they are—knowin' th' law 'n all. I never knew there was so much t'learn about such things. 'Legal descriptions,' they call 'em—you know, namin' the section, township, and range of all th' land we'll be inhabitin'—"

We! The key word that was so important to Rachel. Forgetting Aunt Em's warning, she pulled herself up to hug her knees—unaware that coffee had sloshed from her cup onto the made-down bed and that Aunt Em was wiping it from the faded quilt with a damp rag.

"Do you mean you and Brother Davey have reached a decision? That this will be your home?" Then Cole *had* chosen this site!

Well, a woman's place was by her man's side. *True.* And Cole needed her Davey. *True.* Well, her Davey had decided this land was about as close to heaven as a body could get this side of dying. *Oh, true.* And Cole could come closest to making this into a new city of brotherly love. *Oh, VERY true!*

As Rachel brushed her hair, Aunt Em caught her up on the whereabouts and activities of all the others. Star was sharing a picture book that Cole had been able to find (was Rachel aware that books were as scarce as hen's teeth?). Cole, who had devoted the entire night to "men talk," was addressing the new city council. Who? Well, now, who else but her Davey as chaplain...Buck, city manager...O'Grady ...Farnall...Burnside...Sanders...and all thought it would be fitting and proper to name Judson Lee as Lord Mayor...

The title brought a smile to Rachel's lips. Only Cole could have remembered how important it would be. Yolanda's father would sit on the pinnacle of pride today—

But what was this Aunt Em was saying? Laying her hairbrush down with trembling hands, Rachel turned her eyes away from the small, cracked mirror hung to catch what little light filtered from the front of the tent.

"*Who?*" She asked, hoping her voice would not give away the sudden rise of terror she felt inside. "Who was the man from—from the other group?"

Aunt Em was laying out an unfamiliar, yellow dress and murmuring something about its being Cole's offering to her for today, so she did not turn in response to the question. "The Cowless Column representative? Don't rightly know that his name was mentioned. But he was blackballed—secret ballot, you know. Kind of too bad. Haven't had a chance t' talk with my Davey. Does seem they oughta be represented...wait a minute!"

Slowly Aunt Em turned to face Rachel. "You don't suppose—oh, no, it couldn't be. It just couldn't!"

Rachel turned away for fear her friend would read confirmation of her suspicions. Beyond all doubt the name rejected was that of Julius Doogan. His being a candidate proved what Rachel had hoped was not true. He had friends here besides Agnes Grant. And in shame she realized that she would be counted among them. Oh, why had she let him intimidate her?

18

Accusation

It was good that the first storm of the season had spent itself. The clouds, wrung dry by the winds, moved over the mountain peaks. Only skiffs of fog remained entangled in the mountain range's low summits. Had the main force of the storm continued, the Lee house would never have accommodated the crowd that assembled there for the anticipated day of Thanksgiving. And news of the outside world!

There was confusion as to who was to ride where before departure. Rachel gave up hoping that she would be allowed to travel with Cole; there were too many people and too few wagons. In the end, she herself ended up driving one team and Aunt Em the other, much as they had along the trail. Nothing much has changed, she found herself thinking—an idea which she abandoned quickly. *Everything* had changed on the inside. And that was where change counted. Her faint image of strength in the eyes of the other women had fleshed into reality. She was their established leader through no choosing of her own. Well, it was not their choosing either. It was the Lord's. It occurred to Rachel then that there had been no time for her to share the hearing of His voice with Cole. She doubted that the other men would be receptive to the idea of the Lord's having spoken to a woman. But Cole would understand.

All this she was thinking as the procession of wagons, horseback riders, and running children and dogs tested the rutted road, slickened by last night's rain, in hopes of joining the Lees. Rachel was glad for her experience along the trail.

With their arrival, the day burst into bloom. In the kind of organized confusion that Rachel had grown accustomed to, she watched the men driving pegs for temporary tents and setting up sawhorses for tables beneath the trees as the women unloaded the food. Automatically she helped, with her eyes searching the crowds all the while for Cole. She should have told him about the newcomers, and even warned him about the possible appearance of Julius Doogan. If she and Aunt Em guessed right, by now he knew. She shuddered, wondering what it would all lead to. A promise made in weakness was now a web of deceit.

"You're looking like a cheerful Pilgrim."

"Buck!" Rachel smiled. "I didn't hear you. Here, help me with the buttermilk. Aunt Em churned this morning."

With a practiced roll of the barrel, Buck maneuvered the container of buttermilk from the wagon bed. "You didn't hear me because you were deep in thought. Why so pensive?"

Rachel longed to talk over her concerns about the newcomers with Buck, but a certain reserve held her back. She had hurt Cole at the mine—a hurt she had found no opportunity to make right. She must

not add to it. So she carefully picked up the conversation at its beginning.

"If I look like a cheerful Pilgrim, how can you call
me pensive?" she asked lightly, picking up the jar
of Mr. Lee's coveted "pour."

"Your face looked sober. Your clothes look bright."

"Then I am out of keeping with the day."

"On the contrary, Pilgrims *did* look bright. They
wore colorful clothes. Those grim faces we see staring out of history books belonged to the Puritans."

Buck began rolling the barrel toward the Lee cabin.
Rachel, walking beside him, concentrated on spill-
ing none of the fresh cream she carried—glad
that she did not have to look into Buck's face.
She felt herself to be no Puritan by any sense of the
definition. But she did not want the gentle eyes of
her trusted friend to confirm those feelings.

Yolanda came from the crowd to meet them. She
greeted Buck cordially enough but without the
particular interest that Rachel had hoped to see.
"Over there," she said regarding the barrel, "and
Mr. Lord is looking for you."

Rachel's first thought was that Yolanda and Cole
had met. Her second was to wonder how Yolanda
would greet her. The two of them had not met since
the fateful day at the mine, and it was still unclear
in her own mind exactly what had happened. There
was a third presence, a man, but—

"Your frock is so pretty." Yolanda interrupted her
thoughts as she reached out to take the cream.

A compliment, but no embrace. Just small talk.
"The dress is a gift from Cole," Rachel explained.
"I feel a little out of place wearing something new.
But Aunt Em coaxed, saying it would cheer the
others up—make them a little more apt to accept
some of the dry goods he brought—"

"I doubt that they need coaxing." Yolanda's voice

held an edge. " 'Pride goeth before a fall,' or have you forgotten?"

Something was wrong—something which must be made right. "Yolanda—" Rachel began, then hesitated, praying wordlessly for guidance. "I have forgotten nothing. And most of all, not our friendship. We've always shared everything—"

"Well, we aren't going to share *him!*"

While Rachel struggled to make sense of the words, Yolanda cried out in a low, tortured tone, "You have everything, Rachel—everything! Aunt Em introduced your husband to me. He's handsome and rich—" Yolanda was sobbing now. Rachel reached out to touch her hand in an effort to understand, but Yolanda jerked away. "And there's Buck—it's obvious he adores you. But that's not enough!" Her voice rose so that Rachel feared it would carry to the crowd. "You have to have *him,* too—the only man I can ever love!"

Rachel felt the ground threaten to give way beneath her. Yolanda, her best friend, thought she wanted—Julius Doogan!

19

Tomorrowland

The large group managed somehow to crowd into the Lee cabin. Some distant part of Rachel's mind wondered if they were all holding their breath. But something nearer the forefront pushed aside all other thinking—a fleeting memory that flickered like a newly kindled fire, went out, then reappeared. She tried to concentrate as Yolanda's father read from Ephesians.

"I bow my knees unto the Father of our Lord Jesus Christ, of whom the whole family in heaven and earth is named...."

There was group singing, and Brother Davey prayed. Through it all Rachel struggled with the illusive fragment of recollection. It had to do with a face. A man's face. And the mine. Something about the mine. Something evil...

She was close to putting it together when suddenly she was brought from her reverie by the sharp jab of an elbow in her ribs. "Your turn,"

Abe Lee whispered, suppressing a giggle.

Her turn? For what? Rachel could only stare at the boy blankly. To her immense relief, he came to her rescue. Putting a freckled hand to his mouth, he whispered, "Name somethin' you're grateful for!"

"Friends," she said quickly, feeling the hot blood creep up to stain her neck.

And then the moment was gone. Voices were blending from all corners of the room: "...food...life ...this land...my spiritual children, since the Lord don't see fit sendin' me'n my Davey no family..."

Suddenly she was jolted into reality by hearing her own name mentioned. Someone had praised God "for the likes of Rachel Lord and her help for the poor in spirit!" Rachel looked around the room in a vain effort to locate the speaker, another woman, who had touched her so deeply. But her eyes met Yolanda's instead. And in them she read the hurt of a wounded animal.

I must get to her at once! With that thought, Rachel began the near-impossible task of working her way toward where Yolanda stood. It was no use. The men were seating themselves at the tables inside and outside, and the women were rushing to dish up the food. She was dimly aware that the newcomers of the "Cowless Column," thanks to the help of Cole's group (who knew both parties), were mingling about with a sense of belonging. The plates of the children, she saw, were heaped with mountains of yams and venison stew, more from hunger than greed. One day those gaunt little faces would round out and be energy-filled like Little Star, who, to Rachel's amusement, was paying no heed to the unwritten laws regarding the place of women and children. Taking her plate, she had perched her elfin self in Cole's lap and, with as much mystifying dignity as she did all else, was spooning food into her father's mouth.

Tears of gratitude and appreciation filled Rachel's eyes. *Oh, dear Lord, I have so much—so very much—to thank You for . . . but for now, won't You help me find my friend?*

Her prayer was answered in an unexpected way. As Rachel made a pretense of filling her own plate she caught sight of Yolanda stealing into the little grove of trees behind the barn. And there, lurking in the shadows, was the unmistakable figure of a man slouched against a giant fir.

What had been a flicker of memory burst into flame. Julius Doogan here . . . Julius Doogan at the mine the day she and Yolanda rode up the mountain for the first time . . . leaning over her . . . calling out to her when she fell . . . and, finally, Yolanda's words of astonishment: "How did you know her name?"

Rachel's mind was running nonstop. Was it possible he also was the horseman who looked like a ghost from the Yorkshire moors of a Gothic romance? He was supposed to be in Portland . . . not that one could put any strength in his word.

Why, she wondered, was he spending so much time at the top of Superstition Mountain? And, for that matter, what were Buck and Cole doing there at all? Remembering the stories surrounding the abandoned mine, Rachel shivered with a cold born of fear. But only for a moment. And then suddenly her very being was aflame with another spark from the smoldering embers of memory. Word would have reached Yolanda long before now that Julius Doogan's account of the division of the wagon train far differed from that of other members. Confronted with the truth, together with his being rejected as one of a committee of planners, he would be furious.

All plans would have been thwarted. And he was not a man of reason.

Help. She must get help. Yolanda's very life could be at stake! He would not hesitate to take her hostage...

Hardly aware of her actions, Rachel made her way toward the group of men in which she had last seen Cole. But he was not among them. Maybe she should try to find Buck. No, her first instincts were right. It must be Cole in whom she confided—the whole story. He must know it all.

Hearing the drone of men's voices inside one of the hastily erected tents, Rachel walked quickly toward the entrance. The men inside were talking excitedly, making no effort to keep their voices down. She hesitated, wondering how to go about locating Cole without disrupting the meeting. And in that moment's hesitation she caught sight of a woman's body pressed against the smokehouse. Carefully the woman had positioned herself out of sight of the other women and turned her face to watch the woods from which Yolanda might emerge, while keeping her ear toward the tent for monitoring the men's conversation.

Agnes Grant! Rachel felt a quick flare of indignation which she brought quickly under control. She had accepted long ago that there would always be such women—women whose prime concern in life was probing into the lives of other people and then repeating their findings to any audience willing to listen. Meddling was the driving force of her existence.

Right now the troublesome woman was oddly interested in Yolanda. Undoubtedly she knew of the attraction between her and Julius, for whom she was spying. And, of course, she knew the circumstances of Rachel's marriage...Julius Doogan's advances... her friendship with Buck....all of which she could color to please her fancy. Here was a woman to be pitied—but a woman to be feared as well. Somehow Rachel must lead her away.

In the several seconds that she tried to plot a course of action which would not arouse suspicion, Rachel's ears—like those of Agnes Grant—picked up fragments of the conversation inside the tent. That it had to do with the building of a city there could be no doubt. Schools...churches...and more!

"...impossible to carry wheat overland...should be near the mouth of the river for navigation... high up, though, so as not to wash away at flood stage...after all, in 1848 Portland had two painted houses, one brick one, a handful of cabins, and three frame buildings—unpainted...and look at it now! Why, there are 18 stores, mills set up and running, and a whole line of ships lying along the waterfront. Oregon's yet to name a capital, even though the British, Mexicans, and Russians have hightailed it...could be here...flour mills, sawmills, tanners...general stores...some way of getting the mail...loans...government approval...best get aid now...territory's bound for statehood..."

And then to Rachel's total surprise came the word "nugget." Forgetting both her mission and the other woman's presence, Rachel strained to hear the next words. But hearing was difficult. The men had lowered their voices. She caught a woman's name, *Janet*. No, not a woman. A ship. The ship had reached the mouth of the Willamette River and tied up. *Cargo?* Men, a hundred Oregonians, rich in gold dust and itching to make the country over. *Would they?* Yes, one way or the other. It was a matter of record that three bushels of Oregon apples sold for 300 dollars in California...proving a need for shipping everything movable to better market. The voices died away and then rose again. Rich land might be rich goldfields as well. How could one be sure the scalawag (*did they mention Julius Doogan?*) was telling it straight...carrying gold dust in a tea can there in Portland...saying the hills of Oregon bulged with such? The mountain was not rightly his, of course...another reason for staking claims immediately. Could be Oregon had more gold in her pockets than California...either way, the man was not the rightful owner, Cole having staked claim so long ago...other, a forgery...

Superstition Mountain. They had to be talking about Superstition Mountain. Superstition Mountain and Julius Doogan. First, declaring to have made a strike. Then frightening others away. Filing under false pretenses. A man had to be married before he could hold a square mile...

Rachel's heart refused to believe what her mind was saying. Cole. She must find Cole. *Now!*

She had all but forgotten Agnes Grant. A quick glance at the smokehouse told her Mrs. Grant was gone. Relieved, she took the few steps separating her from the tent, paused to inhale deeply, and then— with the courage she prayed for—moved to stand in full view of the men inside.

For a fleeting second Rachel was able to observe Cole's face unnoticed. What she saw there was a cause of concern. He looked so strained, enigmatic, and reserved. If only she could rush forward and fold her arms around him—

And then Cole's eyes met hers. His entire face changed, as if the very sight of her were food for his hungry soul. Without a word, he rose and began making his way toward her—only to be detained. A name. The unborn city needed a name.

"Tomorrow—Tomorrowland," he murmured, and continued toward Rachel.

20

The Rim of Fire

Outside, Cole took Rachel in his arms, but there was no time for words. A woman's scream alerted the crowd to danger. At the sound of it, Cole's arms dropped to his sides and his eyes searched the hills with practiced caution.

"Get inside," he whispered to Rachel. "It could mean an Indian attack."

Rachel hurried to do his bidding, only to find the doorway blocked with women pouring outside. The scream must have come from elsewhere.

Star. Where was Star? Perhaps she screamed the child's name as she wildly tried to push through the bewildered crowd. Or maybe she prayed. Surely some power other than her own brought the sudden full-bodied hug of Aunt Em, who calmly placed Star in her arms.

"That Aggie!" Aunt Em said in disgust. "Piercin' th' very ears of th' earth with her hysterics!"

"Does the earth have ears, Mother mine?"

How like this wonder child to focus on a pleasing thought instead of possible danger. Rachel held her close, drawing more comfort, she felt, than she gave.

"Oh, yes, Darling," she said, "ears and a mouth—"

"That spews water to make rivers and rainbows. And the earth has grass for hair and a mountain for a nose. God gave the earth a face. Verdad?"

"Verdad," Rachel said, her eyes watching for some sign from Cole. Aunt Em had moved away and was lost among the milling women.

Again the scream, this time followed by excited babbling. And, yes, the voice was indisputedly that of Agnes Grant.

"I saw it—I saw it!" The woman kept yelling in spite of others who tried to quiet her. "The rim of fire—just like before! Right there on the mountain-top—and ain't no good gonna come of it. Somebody's gonna be dyin' t'satisfy th' spirits—somebody evil or we'll be done in fer sure—"

"Shut up, Aggie!" Aunt Em marched up to Agnes Grant, who was either hysterical or, Rachel thought suspiciously, putting on a good act. Cringing before Aunt Em's hand, raised in midair as if to gag her, the woman calmed somewhat.

But not soon enough. Every eye had turned in fear to Superstition Mountain. If the ancient volcano should erupt, lava would flow to the floor of this very valley. Only there was no fire. Not even any smoke. And briefly it appeared that the incident was closed. But Judson Lee had been too long silent.

"A raven!" he boomed, his ruddy face alive with excitement as he pointed a finger at the glossy-black bird circling the peak of Superstition Mountain. "Be ye knowin' what it means?"

Rachel would have felt more comfortable had there been fewer answers. There was a mixture of responses—all spelling doom.

"Th' bird symbolizes greed and trickery!"

"A real devil, it is—"

"Not a devil precise-like—more one o' them message-carryin' vultures from th' Creator to th' world and all its creatures—"

"Exceptin' mankind. Him, the demon'd have wiped from th' face o'th' earth—"

Judson, aware that his words spoken in half-jest had gone out of control, raised a hand for silence. "Now, now—best ye not be speakin' on such matters. Wife here bein' due to deliver! 'Tis a stork we be needin'—not a raven."

Gradually the excitement died except for the mutterings of Agnes Grant. The new child would be marked, she said. No way around it. The whole valley was doomed.

"And them sufferin' worst'll be them that's too blind t'see th' signs...destroyed, that's what... destroyed by th' rim of fire!"

21

Pleased to Present

Some of the brightness had gone from the day. Rachel was relieved when preparations for departure began. Somehow she must arrange for riding back with Cole. The talk between them could no longer be postponed.

But a moment alone with him seemed impossible. People with last-minute questions regarding mail, the filing of claims, and countless other details crowded between them. When at last he caught her eye and signaled for her to stay put, Rachel saw that there were three other men with him. Almost immediately they were beside her.

"This," Cole said without preamble, "is General John Wilkes, candidate for Territorial Governor, Rachel. General, I am pleased to present my wife."

The tall, middle-aged man in uniform smiled, his brown eyes lighting with admiration. Rachel received his compliment graciously, but her mind was elsewhere. How thoughtful of Cole to present the distinguished gentleman to her instead of the other way around. The thrill of pride, rather than the general's compliments, were responsible for the becoming rise of color in her cheeks.

As she turned to greet the second man in the group, Rachel realized that some kind of kinship had been established between General Wilkes and her husband—something which would be invaluable as Cole pursued his dream. Behind the man's kindly smile she had sensed the hum of machinery and a meshing of gears, from which she drew comfort.

"And United States Marshal Hunt," Cole was saying.

The marshal extended his hand. Older, she guessed, and less inclined to smile. But his handshake was hearty. Here was another strong ally for her husband, and one equally distinguished. Rachel was suddenly glad that she had chosen to wear the yellow dress.

In the next moment she was wondering if the new dress—cotton though it was—would make the third man in the party uncomfortable.

"Name's Burt Clemmons," the man in faded overalls said without waiting for an introduction. "I'm a wheat-plantin' man...worked barefooted after my shoes give out. Had its advantages, though. Me, I can walk on thorns and nettles with the thick pads I've developed—"

When Rachel would have kept her face averted to avoid embarrassing him, Burt Clemmons stuck out a bare foot proudly.

Rachel found herself liking the man for his simplicity. To him, a pair of moccasins belonged to the more wealthy, she supposed. She smiled and was rewarded by a mischievous grin. She felt a new surge of pride in Cole and respect for his chosen colleagues who in their "store-bought" clothes recognized the value of opinions expressed by a man who could not afford to wear them. It was another example of the kind of togetherness she was learning to expect here on the frontier. These Portland city planners were cut from similar cloth.

All the same, Rachel felt a keen sense of disappointment when Cole explained that he would travel with the three man back to camp. Plans must be made, he told her, on getting up some immediate shelter. Brother Davey would need additional time with the council, so perhaps she and Aunt Em could take one wagon and allow the men to have the other.

Rachel nodded, not trusting her voice for fear her feelings would show. The three men did not move on, so Cole was only able to squeeze her fingertips in appreciation, making sure, she supposed, that the gesture went unobserved.

"You were wonderful," he whispered, his lips hardly moving. And then the group was gone.

I was wonderful. I am always "wonderful." And there it ends. Rachel realized that her disappointment had turned to bitterness. Once the words would have thrilled her through and through. Now she wondered if she would ever be more to Cole than a "wonderful" hostess he was pleased to present!

22

Dearly Beloved

Rachel had climbed into the springseat to sit beside Aunt Em when she caught sight of Yolanda. She was standing inside a circle of older women who were admiring the bolts of gingham and calico they had divided among themselves. Holding a swath of red plaid against her face, Yolanda looked as if all were normal. But there was melancholy in her usually snapping eyes, and her smile looked painted on. At least Yolanda was safe.

Following Rachel's gaze, Aunt Em clucked her tongue. But the words she said were, "Giddyup, boys. Time fer yer oats!"

When they were underway, Aunt Em turned to Rachel. "I was right glad Star stood her ground 'bout ridin' with her daddy. Gonna push the cause of women ahead one day, that one. But fer now, Dearie, out with it!"

Rachel opened her mouth, clamped it shut, then opened it again. Suddenly she found herself sharing the whole weight of her problem with the kindly sympathy beside her. By the time she finished, there was very little Aunt Em did not know—except for some of the finer points.

"I really don't know what to think—" Rachel said, her irritation having given way to desperation.

"Well, *I* know what t'think. You and Cole are in need of time alone—jest th' two of you, th' way th' good Lord intended it t'be! Now, now—no backtalk. Your openin' up like that entitles me t'speak on th' matter. Besides which, I've laid claims on you as my daughter-in-spirit." Capably, Aunt Em pulled the lines to the right, guiding the team away from a deep rut, and then resumed, "My Davey 'n me'll keep Star so's I can make her a dress. . ."

If Aunt Em went on talking, Rachel did not hear. The problems here could wait. Hers and Cole's could not.

It was dusk when the wagons reached camp. Cole lifted a sleeping Star gently from the wagon and took her into the tent, motioning for Rachel to follow. There in the shadows he drew her close and bent to kiss her with a soft-sweet urgency that took her breath away.

"Oh, Cole, I—I—will you take me with you?" Rachel whispered as she had whispered once before when she made what she knew must be an immodest plea for Colby Lord to help her escape her bullying father.

And his answer now, as it was then, came. "I couldn't leave without you."

In no time at all they were speeding away. Rachel, leaning against the familiar strength of his chest, felt the stirring spirit of deja vu which she knew Cole had intended. The months between might never have been. The two of them were escaping this world as they had escaped that one. Her skirt billowed outward as the black stallion headed into an even blacker night. Fog loosened her hair and the wind once again wrapped it around the face of the man behind her. Only this time he was her husband. Where they were going did not matter. She was a girl again. And yet she was a woman. Both in love with the same man. So much in love that all things were made new . . .

They must have come upon the inn quite suddenly. One moment she and Cole were wrapped in the black velvet sleeves of night. The next, a circle of light—like a fallen moon—illuminated a rambling, unpainted building, leaning against the mountainside.

"Welcome to Wayside Inn," Cole said, helping her to the ground. "This is the only stopover between here and the city—unless one has friends."

Which Cole had, Rachel remembered thinking in gratitude. Then she heard him explaining to a white-haired man in a flannel gown and nightcap that they would be staying only one night. He had tethered Hannibal, and if the stableboy would take over from there—yes, breakfast at six. Then, accepting a lighted candle from the innkeeper, Cole led her up the rickety stairs.

"Hungry?" Cole asked as the door of the tiny room creaked shut behind them.

Rachel shook her head. The motion brought her hair tumbling about her face. For a moment she stood staring sightlessly at the bare walls around her, unaware of the beautiful picture she made— flushed with happiness, her dark-fringed lashes becoming crescents against her cheeks in the soft glow of the candlelight. But Cole was very much aware.

"Nervous?" His voice trembled as he moved toward her.

Again, the shake of her head. And then the sudden holding out of her arms and being swept into the arms of the man with whom she hoped to spend an eternity.

"Dearly beloved," he whispered.

Dearly beloved. Rachel would cherish the words forever. Now they held a deeper meaning than when Brother Davey singsonged through the meaningless ceremony. Now they sent her afloat with love and wonder. From this day forward the two of them were a part of each other, belonging forever . . .

It was not yet dawn when Rachel awoke. When she stirred, Cole took her in his arms. "Good morning, Bunny Face!"

It was his pet name for her on the Oregon Trail. "How can you see I'm wrinkling my nose?"

"I have honeymoon eyes. Honeymoon eyes are bright and can see through the dark—"

His words were never finished. Neither was there time for telling him what was so vital to them and their friends. A soft knock interrupted. Mr. Lord's horse was ready. Breakfast was laid. A young man was here to meet Mrs. Lord. *Another goodbye!*

23

Rumors of War

Rachel was firmly cheerful when she returned to the settlement. Life must go on. All about her was the sound of singing saws and the crash of falling trees. Such sounds meant that the men were following the plans laid out Thanksgiving. Any day now the winter rains could set in, and the tents had seen their best days on the trail. It would take time. Rachel only hoped there was enough.

But, Rachel realized as she walked out to examine the foundations of the quarters some two weeks after her one night with Cole, everything worthwhile took patience—time and space. With pleasure she thought of her marriage—how she and Cole, two separate entities, each had allowed the other a "self," slowly forming a common thread, strong and lasting, neither overwhelming nor underwhelming, but allowing each other to grow.

Maybe God had planned it this way, holding them apart just long enough to make them see the value of listening and feeling the individual rhythms of other beings before expecting them to harmonize. After all, there were three groups who must learn to live together here. If they could see examples of flexible leaders, maybe they could withstand together the push and pull that eternally takes place between human beings. Communities must grow gradually into cities just as babies grow to adulthood.

Thinking of this, Rachel realized she must check on Mrs. Lee. Wasn't the baby overdue? She had neither seen nor heard from Yolanda. And Julius Doogan's surprising failure to show up to claim his "rightful place" was more cause for alarm than his presence would have been. At least, then things would have been out in the open.

Deep in thought, Rachel was unaware that Buck had joined her until he spoke. "Meet with your approval?"

"Actually, I was thinking more than looking," she admitted. But she was looking now. And what she saw surprised her. The layout before her looked like a small village. "I don't understand. Weren't there claims filed? And I had expected—well, something far different—"

"A house on each homestead?"

"Well, yes—homes like the Lees have." Where was the tidy little cabin with frilly curtains and morning glories twining around the windows—the honeymoon cottage she and Cole would share? Clenching her teeth to hide her disappointment, Rachel started to murmur something, then stopped, an instinctive fear gripping her heart.

"It's a fort, isn't it?" Her words were a whisper.

"It's the beginnings of a city, Rachel. Proving the individual claims takes time. Cole felt that the work would go faster this way. Families can occupy the buildings and vacate as they complete their cabins—" Buck did not meet her eyes.

"This is the land grant? Under what terms?"

Buck smiled. "You are becoming quite an entrepreneur! My understanding is that there must be a school of sorts, in case," Buck looked meaningfully at her, "we can convince certain parties to oblige."

He was asking her to teach? Why, the idea was preposterous—or was it? "I have no certificate—"

Buck relaxed visibly. Rachel realized then that he had been assigned to the job of approaching her. "With your background—as a matter of fact, it's probably arranged by now. Our visitors were to give the problem priority. And you'll need help. Mr. Lee says you tutored his daughter—"

"Her name's Yolanda," Rachel said softly.

Buck's face reddened. "Yolanda," he repeated. "Will you solicit her help?"

"I'll try," she promised. "But she's very busy at home and—"

"She's wrestling with some other problems as well? It's the young man, isn't it? How could he love her and make her so miserable?"

"Young man," Buck had said. It struck Rachel for the first time that Buck was unaware of his identity. She dug back into her mind trying to recall if either Buck or she herself had made mention of Julius Doogan's name. No, she was sure they had not. They had spoken of him in pronouns.

Realizing she was tardy with an answer, Rachel promised to see Yolanda. Buck was pleased and said that Aunt Em had volunteered to resume the Bible studies for children and that Brother Davey was more than pleased to be allowed to preach.

Then it was all settled? No, it was not settled at all. Something was still troubling Rachel.

"The design of these buildings still reminds me of a fort. Are you sure you're telling me everything?"

"It would serve the purpose—in case of a raid—"

Raid. *Indian* raid! The very words chilled her blood. "Is there a real threat, Buck? Tell me the truth!"

Buck looked at her a little sadly. "There's always a threat, Rachel. And it's best to be prepared. Being unprepared was the problem when I lost Amanda—on our wedding day."

"Oh, Buck, I didn't know—I'm so sorry—" Rachel reached out her hand and he took it, squeezing hard.

"It's all right, Rachel. That was a long time ago—but I can't lose those I love again. Once was all I could stand." He hesitated as if wondering whether to continue, and when he spoke there was trembling in his voice. "There's a rumor that the Indians are riled by the white man's presence at Superstition Mountain—also that they believe we have one of their children—"

"*Star!* Oh, dear God, no!" Rachel cried out.

24

Shadows of the Mountain

It seemed to Rachel that the shadows of Superstition Mountain grew longer. Even as the horseshoe of log buildings took shape, a certain dark surrounded it. She noted in particular that the tallest building, with a hewed-out cross rising higher than the others, as if reaching for light, was all but lost in shadow. So even the house of God was not immune, Rachel thought with a shudder.

She herself felt a certain depression, and she desperately tried to shake off the feeling. It was only natural that she would be lonely for her husband. And certainly what Buck had said put her nerves on edge. Being careful to create no more anxiety than existed in the settlement already, Rachel alerted Aunt Em and Brother Davey. The three of them kept Star in sight at all times. There was nothing to be done about preventing an Indian attack—nothing except hope and pray that it never happened.

The people of the settlement busied themselves

with staying ahead of the winter rains. They did not discuss the possibility of a raid. The threat just hung there like a cloud under which they all must live. But there were other rumors. The words of Agnes Grant now began to spread like wildfire.

And the Scots among them kept the rumors alive. Somebody had seen "a horse without no rider." Another saw vapors rising like smoke signals "at morn-gloam time, elsewise when it's dusty-dark." And the raven—always the raven!

More than once Rachel would walk into a group unexpectedly and hear them recalling old legends. These happenings were "nigh on" like those preceding the cave-in that buried all the men alive. Warnings, they were. And then, seeing Rachel, the group would change the subject quickly.

Rachel felt helpless in the face of growing unrest. How did one stop such nonsense? They all seemed to be waiting—almost willing—for something to happen.

It was seeing the more venturesome men ride toward the mountain after the day's work was done that brought Rachel to a sudden decision. She would ride over to the Lee homestead in hopes of having a talk with Yolanda. If they could get some sort of classes underway, perhaps the interest in the mountain would fade.

On the way, she saw several women poking around the trail leading to the mountain. Some of them had their children along. She hesitated and then pulled up alongside them.

"Good news!" she said more brightly than she felt. "I have agreed to resume classes for the children."

There was instant interest. But books? Well, there were the Bibles that Cole brought, Rachel said, quickly improvising. She had a *Poor Richard's Almanac*. And it took no textbook for ciphering or morals and manners. Later there would be more books, she was sure.

As Rachel rode away, she saw that the women had turned back toward camp, chatting excitedly among themselves. She hoped Yolanda would be as easy to convince.

Rachel slowed the horse. These mothers loved their children. Loving them meant wanting the best for them. And so they were no longer afraid.

" 'There is no fear in love.' " Rachel murmured the words of John aloud, tasting the multi-dimensional beauty of God's promise. Unbidden came the memory of the one night she and Cole had shared at the inn. Shyly, on tentative feet the memory came at first. Then, with a honeycombed sweetness, it rushed in as if all the time in the world would never be enough to make up for that which they had lost.

Darling! Oh, Darling... her heart cried out, remembering. . . .

Was she nervous, Cole had asked. *Nervous?* Did the word properly describe her feelings? Everything had been so wrong. The time. The place. And yet it had been so *right*. Rachel smiled with misty eyes, remembering her mother's genteel reminders on bridal behavior. The bride should precede the groom to the bridal chambers, preparing for his knock. Of course, it would have been unheard of that a newly wedded couple should arrive at midnight astride a stallion! So, what could the further departure of carrying a flickering candle up a rickety stairway together matter? She was excited, exhilarated, and, yes, *of course*, she was nervous!

. . . Until Cole closed the door behind them and took her tenderly into his arms. Then the excitement of the night changed. He was no longer the hand-some stranger with whom she rode against the wind. He was her husband, whose sweetness and love caused the cup of her heart to overflow. What could be more exciting than that?

"Dearly beloved..." Cole had whispered the words over and over, dissipating her fear like the morning sun wiped away the fog. "Dearly beloved..." Rachel had wanted to answer him back but her heart was too full. She had loved him before. But never like this. She was a part of him. He was a part of her. Belonging. Forever belonging...

Time, thief though it was, could never steal those hours. It could only interrupt their honeymoon. "Honeymoon eyes!" The memory of Cole's words brought a needed laugh to Rachel's throat. He had honeymoon eyes, he had teased in the intimacy of the dawn. And honeymoon eyes could see through the darkness. Ultimately, that kind of vision would bring him back to her. That thought must sustain her.

Just as it must sustain Cole. She remembered now that he had been awake when first she stirred on the morning of their parting. Her first clear memory was his calling her "Bunny Face." But, stumbling into the world of the waking, she remembered now that Cole had said something about watching over her while she slept...how innocent she looked, how happy...in love, he said, with the "right man" and with life....

Cole, wonderful Cole, who would watch over her forever!

There was a great deal of excitement at the Lees. Abe had gone with his father to help with the building of the "village." In his absence, the rest of the clan was having a heyday with what otherwise would have been a tedious task of threshing out the cured grain.

Bart, the oldest of the group left behind, saw

Rachel first. At his warning, "Company's here!" the other nine boys snapped to attention.

"Hello, men!" Rachel smiled. At the sign of her friendliness, the boys began chattering like a flock of magpies. Pa would be so proud. First, they had turned the calves into the corral and let them trample out the grain...had to keep 'em moving or the fool critters would eat instead of trampling. 'Course they went faster if one of them caught a young heifer by the tail...then she'd bawl and try gettin' away, makin' the tail-holder take steps ten feet long! This would start the rest of 'em going full tilt, so the grain got ground...

The boys were laughing so hard at their own stories that they had to pause for breath. Rachel, laughing with them, looked around. Her eyes fastened on a giant fir tree, and there she saw the old coffee mill she remembered so well fastened to the trunk. The boys, now in control, followed Rachel's gaze.

"I'm mostly the grinder," volunteered Phil (who looked too small to reach the handle). "Hafta grind all the wheat for the bread Ma bakes. I let the little 'uns blow away the chaff. Takes 'em all to huff and puff it out!"

"Have you read that story—the one about the three little pigs—"

"And the ole wolf that huffed and puffed? We got no books, but Yolanda's told us," Chris answered.

"Do you like Bible stories, too?"

There was a unanimous "Yes!"

Rachel told them her plans then, and was rewarded by a look of awe on their faces. "We never been to school," said Jeremiah. "Ma's poorly. She's sure gonna be glad to see you."

Rachel turned toward the house. Then one of the boys called out a warning not to get "treed" by one of Pa's Spanish cows. They were cheaper, you know, but downright dangerous.

Rachel, casting a wary eye at the motley herd, believed the boy. The long-horned cows were thin and angry-eyed. It was easy to see that they were as wild as deer. She picked up her skirts and ran the rest of the distance. The horse, forgotten, followed—nibbling grass on either side.

Listening to the Lee children had been refreshing. Rachel had grown excited over the adventure that lay ahead with organizing some sort of school for them and the other children of the settlement. At first she had felt she had little to offer, but now she realized differently. That these children had never been to school was incredible. And yet it was understandable. Where would they have gone for instruction? Well, the Lord was certainly using her! Rachel felt a sort of giddy exhilaration. And for the moment the shadows lifted.

But they descended again inside the Lee house. Nola Lee, looking thin in spite of the big burden she carried, did not rise from the sprint-oak chair where she sat sewing minute pieces together for a quilt. Instead, she motioned Rachel inside with a wan smile. "Think I'll be needin' a granny-woman soon." Her voice was weak. "You'll excuse me, dear Rachel?"

"Of course!" Rachel assured her. "And I want to see your new quilt anyway."

But it was not quilts that Nola Lee wished to discuss. It was Yolanda. Hardly aware of Rachel's embrace, she said sadly, "My daughter has disappeared."

25

An Outward Calm

Two weeks slipped by. Rachel had forced herself into a routine which, she hoped, would be helpful to the others who felt so uncertain about the future—and preserve her own sanity. The women, and occasionally some of the men, were relying on her more and more. There were times when she wondered if she had not become more involved with business matters than Cole himself.

But it was good to be busy, to keep involved—and to avoid thinking as much as possible. When she felt bone-weary (and the times were more and more frequent), Rachel would steal away for a quiet time with the Lord. Only He understood that there were days when she felt she simply could not go on.

Most of the days were overcast now. The air had a chill to it. And there were frequent periods of light rain. The tents provided little protection, and so many of the settlers had come down with the grippe that Aunt Em's home remedies were in popular demand. . .this tea "fer sweatin' you". . .that tea "fer clearin' you out". . .and everybody "knowed whey poured off buttermilk'll take care o' th' bellyache." Some complained that her medicines were not working. Aunt Em promptly retorted, "We got nothin' else—'ceptin' prayer."

All the while the seemingly tireless woman kept an eye on Rachel's *Almanac*. "All signs bein' right, th' twelfth—and last, let us be hopin'—little Lee's past due. It's right worried 'bout Nola, I am."

Rachel was worried, too—about the weary-looking woman and her daughter's still-unexplained disappearance. In sharing the frightening news with Aunt Em, Rachel had suggested that it be kept quiet. It would only fan the spark of unrest that lay buried dangerously near the surface of the settlers' temporary calm.

But there was more. Rachel put no strength in the so-called "signs." No strength either in the strange goings-on near the mysterious mountain. At least she did not *think* she did. On the other hand, secretly she wondered if her own mind were not crying out "Wolf!" too many times. She had let fear be her master when Julius Doogan reappeared. . . again when his former followers came. Then there was Yolanda's disappearance on Thanksgiving, and her own panic. At present she was carrying the burden of Yolanda's leaving—obviously to be with Julius Doogan. . .the whispers of the "dark child" who might be riling the Indians. . .and fear of an Indian attack and allowing it to steal away her reason. None of these things had happened—*yet*! So, lest she be as guilty as those who delved in superstition, Rachel tried to put the dark imaginings from her mind, knowing all the while that in a very real sense she was only sublimating them. One day they would surface.

"But You will be there, won't You, Lord?" Rachel whispered over and over as she carried on with outward calm.

And she prayed that Cole would soon be here, too. There had been no word from him, and the splendor of their one night together was but a fragile dream. "Tomorrowland," Cole had said when asked to christen the city-to-be. Rachel smiled at the memory. Always it would be their secret that Cole was thinking of the timing of their planned togetherness when he absently said the word—which made it all the more precious to Rachel. *Tomorrow!* While she drove her physical self to a state of near-exhaustion, her heart lived in that bright tomorrow.

• • •

The week before Christmas, Rachel began classes. The men had split logs and made them into benches for the "Meeting House," which would serve as a school on weekdays and a church on Sundays. Thoughtfully, they erected a giant black bell, salvaged from the ruins of an Indian massacre at the Waiilatpu Mission School. Agnes Grant took advantage of the gesture and went about muttering darkly, "History repeats itself, fer sure!" Excited about their children's education, few people paid much attention to her. That pleased Rachel immeasurably. She was glad that she herself had resisted the temptation of asking the woman if she knew of Yolanda's whereabouts. Agnes Grant might know. But putting rumors and gossip to rest was of vital importance.

"What in the world am I going to do with you all?" Rachel asked in amazement when she saw every crude bench crowded with squeezed-together children of all ages and more standing in back—their faces clouded with disappointment the day classes began.

"Could we learn each other?" The question came from a girl with shining eyes. Rachel judged her age at 12 or 13.

"Yes," Rachel said slowly. "Yes, I think we could *teach* one another."

The shine did not go out of the girl's eyes as she corrected herself on the verb. There, Rachel decided, was Teacher Number One, with some proper coaching.

Rachel asked her name and found that it was Nita Marie. "Nita Marie, will you help me distribute the Bibles?"

Nita Marie proudly obliged. Rachel was in the midst of calling the younger children up to the crude table which was to serve as a desk when Judson Lee, his very presence seeming to push aside all others and to fill the room, trooped in. His sons, marching in a military row, followed.

"As Lord Mayor, I thought it be wise I check on matters," Mr. Lee announced for all to hear. Then to Rachel he said, "Ye be in need o' more benches, 'tis plain t'see."

"And another teacher." The moment she said it, Rachel could have bitten her tongue. He knew she meant Yolanda.

Immediately Mr. Lee issued a command. "Abraham, be livin' up t'your name, me boy! Th' Father-of-many's responsible fer th' good of all. Take your brothers and git sawin'. *Now!* Be ye deaf?"

Rachel's heart was heavy for the man. The anger in his voice revealed the inner hurt of his daughter's disappearance. After a look at Rachel's face, he turned away.

Rachel, busily shepherding the smaller children

who obediently had clustered about her, whispered, "I'm sorry."

"*Sorry!*" The word was a bellow he must have borrowed from one of his Spanish cows. "I'll tell ye who be sorry! That gal—that's who—runnin' away like unto an odious woman. Best she not come crawlin' back bearin' a woods colt!"

Rachel had no idea what a "woods colt" meant. But she could guess it meant a child born out of wedlock. The very thought of it formed an icicle near her heart. An icicle which melted into unshed tears. Poor Yolanda. And poor Mr. Lee. There was more to grieve about than he could imagine if his daughter (clearly the apple of his eye, although it was "womanish" not to prefer the male of the species) was, as Rachel suspected, with Julius. How could she explain to a remorseful father—except to say that many women were guilty of loving the wrong man?

Soon school, like Rachel's life, settled into a routine. Each morning she conducted chapel, opening and closing with prayer. The children loved to sing. Using the words of hymns, patriotic songs, nursery rhymes, and an increasing number of Bible verses, she made charts on any paper she could find. The boys, as well as the girls, were pathetically eager to learn to read. For that reason they found no quarrel with her inadequate supplies.

And then there was Star. The child truly lived up to her name, seeming to light every corner of the dark room. And certainly it needed lighting! There were squares cut for windows, but there was no glass. So it was necessary to close the openings temporarily with patches of canvas from the rotting tents. As yet there was no floor either, so Rachel's feet were pinched with cold. When she would have agonized, she looked at the countless children who were barefoot—thankful that Star had moccasins. The fireplace was always hungry. Thank goodness, the men provided wood to satisfy its appetite. The wide-open mouth gave an illusion of warmth and a measure of light. Star, in her corner, furnished the rest. In English. In Spanish. And the language of love!

Tirelessly, the wisp of a child drew pictures and told stories, combining truth and a fertile imagination. She must have been born reading, Rachel marveled. Now and then a strange, faraway look crossed the pixie face. But for the most part, Star, like her mother, affected an outward calm.

26

Warmth of a Star

Rachel stood outside her tent scanning the skies with the hope of gathering the spirit of Christmas from the galaxies overhead. Even as she watched, one star seemed to come closer to earth than all the rest—so close she felt she could reach out and warm her cold hands by its beams. But it was too far away, too far to warm her hands. Neither could a star warm her heart. *Oh, Cole. . . Cole. . . how long?*

Somewhere in the distance there was the lonely cry of a wolf. In search of food, or of his mate? Was his life, like her own, a constellation of burnt-out stars?

Sometimes Rachel wondered if her memories of her husband were grounded in fact or fantasy. There had been so little time together. And did they, even then, reveal themselves to each other entirely? She did not and she doubted if he did. Always they were on guard—each forcing a smile neither felt in their hearts. Protecting one another as it were from hurt, because another parting always waited in the wings. Inside, she had changed. Rachel wondered how much Cole had changed, too. Permanence, the thing she coveted, was not for them. And without it, they could not be changing together.

Memories were not enough. And now, truthfully, dreams were not enough either! She needed Cole in the flesh. To touch him. To smooth his hair. Trace his eyebrows, his cheekbones, his lips—those firm, beautiful lips that tasted suspiciously of salt in their last goodbye. She needed his arms around her. His body against hers as he whispered a little prayer into her hair as she drifted off to sleep. His arms around her, his lips feathering little kisses in the hollow of her neck, as she floated in for a soft landing from the world of dreams each morning. She needed the joy-shine of his eyes when he looked at her, the warm glory of their love, their togetherness. And she needed it *now*! Rachel shook her head to clear away the dreams. Stop *moping*, she scolded herself, wiping away the tears.

Wearily she turned back. She could take comfort at least in Buck's news that they would be moving into the temporary quarters tomorrow. She was thankful for the shelter of the "village" (still a fortress to her). But Rachel found it impossible to share the excitement which the others expressed. Home to her was a cottage in a fern-shadowed dell . . . near to the townsite so Cole could follow his dream . . . while she followed hers, surrounding him with love and children . . .

Moving took place on schedule. There was very little to move. And all of the joined-together cabins looked amazingly alike once the washstands were fitted into the corners, a homemade table placed in the center, and a few hide-bottom chairs scattered here and there. Braided rugs on the bare-ground floors added brightness to the otherwise-cheerless rooms, their windows boarded up like sightless eyes.

The families were as crowded as the cabins—as many as a dozen members in some of them, Rachel guessed—elbowing one another for space. Not even one of her freckles would fit between!

"What'll we do if company comes?" One of the Farnall twins wondered aloud.

The other giggled. "Pull ourselves a feather tick off'n Mama's bed. She'd never miss it!" he said.

That just about summed up the good-natured philosophy that prevailed, Rachel thought gratefully. Looking forward to a better tomorrow, as she herself was, they simply followed Brother Davey's suggestion of "lettin' today's problems be sufficient unto theirselves—'cause bigger ones might be comin'!"

At least, thinking of the bigger ones was postponed. The frightening rumors no longer ran rampant. Or, at least, they did not reach Rachel's ears. Apparently few knew of Yolanda's disappearance. When Judson spoke of her it was as if his daughter were dead.

• • •

It was Friday, the day before Christmas Eve. Rachel awoke with a feeling of something left undone. Of course, a Christmas program! Small wonder she had given the matter no thought with all she had on her mind. Still, children were children. They deserved better.

There was to be a worship service tomorrow night in the Meeting House. With her help, could the children prepare a small program? It would take all day rehearsing—a blessing she welcomed, as it would keep her from thinking, from remembering that it was Christmas and that families should be together. She, like the children, deserved better. A tear slid down her cheek as she hurriedly dressed and brushed her hair before awakening Star.

The children were delighted with the idea of the program, and their suggestions were surprisingly practical.

"We can sing 'Silent Night' and let Star sing one verse in Mexican" (*Spanish*, but, yes, that was fine, Rachel said). "I'll bring mistletoe"..."And we'll gather boughs...."

"But, Mother Mine, there has to be a bambino, the Baby Jesus." Star's voice, always to Rachel's ears carrying the ring of silver spoons, rose above the din of voices.

"There's no time to practice—" Rachel protested weakly, only to be told by a loud chorus that Star could *draw* the manger scene. Already they were surrounding her with paper and chalk.

Rachel wondered later how she got through the day, managing to direct, to smile, to force some enthusiasm into her voice when her heart was as heavy as melted-down lead.

● ● ●

Rachel found herself surrounded with children, their eyes shining and their cheeks made rosy from scrubbing. The heavy rain could not dampen the spirit of the program.

Every woman in the settlement must have brought candles. The great room was aglow, causing shadows to dance across the touchingly beautiful drawing of Mary and Joseph leaning over the Christ Child in His manger bed. The scent of evergreens was sweeter than the frankincense and myrrh could possibly have been. And could an angel choir sing more sweetly?

Caught up in the scene, Rachel identified with Mary, the little peasant girl who must have been confused and afraid as she herself so often was. But Mary had pondered those doubts in her heart. Rachel thought of Nola Lee, whose deliverance was past due. A worry, yes, but at least she would have a midwife and caring family and friends. Mary had nobody. Yet she had brought the Son of God to save a dying world. It was a timeless story, old but made new by something Rachel could not identify. With all her heart she wished that Cole were here to share this mysterious moment.

And then Star unexpectedly stood and, on tiptoe, made her way through the crowd to stand beside her drawing.

"Once upon a time," she told a silent audience, "in la ciudad of Bethlehem, a Baby comed—*came*—to bring a basket of love. De que color? I do not know. But I think He was like my coat of many colors. Then all who looked saw a favorite color—all of them beautiful."

Rachel, choked with emotion, reached out her arms to receive her child, feeling the warmth of a special star.

27

The Medicine Man

Rachel awoke from a beautiful dream. A smile curved her lips at the memory of having walked with Cole beneath a Christmas moon. But it was not the moon that had made the dream world bright and iridescent. It was the light of the love stretched between them—gossamer-thin but promise-filled. *Tomorrowland*...

She was still floating weightlessly when there came the chime of bells. Christmas bells...music of the spheres...

And then she realized it was the bell of the Meeting House. Oh, yes, the early Christmas service...

The contours of Cole's face faded. His intense gray-green eyes reached into her heart for one moment. Then they too went into the recesses of her mind. She was reluctantly back in the world of *today*—a world filled with a strange foreboding.

Suddenly something inside Rachel snapped to

attention. Wide awake now, she realized that there was no music in the ring of the bell, not even a welcome—just an incessant clang of iron against iron that warned of danger.

Fumbling in the darkness for her clothes, she dressed quickly and ran outside, where already a crowd had gathered. At first it was hard to make sense of anything. There were too many voices trying to be heard above the ringing of the bell. By pushing and pleading, Rachel finally made her way into the Meeting House. It, too, was crowded. But some of the men had brought lanterns, and by their dim light Rachel could make out a cluster of Lee children. And that was Goliath (or "Golly," as he chose to be called away from home) hanging onto the bell rope, his body suspended in midair as he swung back and forth.

"Th' baby—th' baby—" he was screaming incoherently.

"Abe, Bart, Dave, Phil, Issie, Jerry—and you, too, Golly—pay attention to me!" Rachel called out in her best schoolteacher voice. "Calm down and we will help—"

"Sure will!" Brother Davey said supportively at her elbow. "My Emmy Gal—her bein' Miz Galloway, that is—is all packed 'n ready fer th' delivery—"

From all directions came offers to help. But the boy, who had stopped swinging at Rachel's command, suddenly resumed. It was the eldest son, Abe, who spoke then. "We come to tell you we've got us another sister. Pa and me was comin' for Aunt Em here—"

"Then," Bart interrupted, "things got bad—real bad for our ma—"

"And we don't know 'bout bornin' babies," Dave said shyly, "leastwise, not *girl* babies!"

There was a small ripple of laughter followed by

relieved voices which drowned out some of the children's words. Rachel, feeling a little uneasy in spite of the obvious good news, was relieved when Buck came to stand beside her.

"Friends!" His deep voice called the crowd to order. "I think we owe it to the boys to listen to their story. Abe, you're the oldest. You first."

"He warn't—*wasn't*—there!" Bart objected. "Me 'n th' rest saw him—helped some, too, we did—"

"*Him*, Bart?" Rachel's tone warned the boy. If this was going to be one of those stories of Santa Claus—

"Th' doctor! Th' medicine man..."

The ten boys were all talking at once again. Rachel could make no sense of anything they said. She only knew that no Indian was going to offer assistance. That made less sense than the Santa Claus story! *Who then could have—*

She could get no farther with the thought. The mood of the crowd had changed. Rachel realized then that Agnes Grant was screaming hysterically, "I told you...I told you...all them other signs... and now this final one...th' comin' of th' medicine man..."

28

Frightening Identity

There was no reason for a Christmas recess. At least, the council and parents decided there was not, since home and school were synonymous. Rachel would have welcomed one. She was so weary, and there was so much that she would like to examine in an effort to help her find the missing pieces of the puzzle of her own life and the events of the wide valley below Superstition Mountain.

One of the missing pieces concerned the strange stories of the "medicine man." During the week following the baby's birth ("Callie" was her name), Rachel questioned the Lee boys about the man who assisted their mother. Each gave a different account. If one put together a composite, Rachel thought wryly, the result would be a tall man with short legs and black hair (or was it yellow? See, he was wearing a hat—*over* his headdress of feathers). His eyes were hidden by a beard. And the beard was hidden by a mask...

Knowing that the children had been scared out of their wits and their mother in pain-induced delirium, Rachel began to doubt if she would ever know the truth.

"What do you make of it?" she asked Aunt Em.

Emmaline Galloway knitted one and pearled two on a sweater she was making for Callie before answering. Then, pursing her lips, she said softly, "Let's not be makin' too much of them scare stories Aggie's toutin'. That woman'd try sweepin' sunshine off the roof with a broom!"

"I wasn't thinking of her," Rachel said, which was only partially true. "I meant the identity of the—"

She paused, stopped by something which had flickered in her memory. But try as she would, no recall would come.

"Medicine man?" Aunt Em finished for her. "Well, I figger it's a made-up tale, which ain't likely—or I'm guessin' it could be—"

This time it was she who hesitated—which was fine. For Rachel felt herself drifting into the kind of darkness that lies below the conscious mind. She was on a mountaintop...then floating down. Consciousness stirred, and a pale light began seeping through the sheer curtains of her mind. It was warm, and there was the smell of wilting flowers and wool...then something sharply aromatic that snatched the very breath from her nostrils. *Ammonia!* And a man's face...

"Julius Doogan," she whispered as if in a trance.

Aunt Em bit off a thread before answering. "Probably," she said without emotion. "Well, no matter what else he's up to, the Lord'd have us credit him with one good deed."

29

A Love to Lean On

Rachel left her schoolwork undone and, settling Star and her coloring book with the Galloways, made a quick trip to see the new baby. Nola Lee, whose face still looked haggard but whose spirits were revived, placed Callie in Rachel's arms.

"Don't she remind you of Yolanda at that age?"

Rachel laughed against the warmth of the baby's round, fuzzy head. "Yolanda and I are the same age. Remember?"

"I'm sorry," the older woman murmured. "It's just that I've been cooped up so long and in need of another woman's company . . . and that I miss my daughter so much . . ."

Rachel, aware that Mr. Lee was splitting kindling near the back door, asked quickly if there had been any word. Yolanda's mother shook her head sadly just as her husband entered.

The big Scotsman boomed praises of his latest offspring and, to Rachel's surprise, to "Wife here who born 'er." There was no mention of the mysterious medicine man, leaving Rachel to wonder if he presumed that one of the beings from his spirit-world had aided. Or had he feared losing this daughter too?

A new year was beginning, Rachel remembered as she rode back. Maybe it would be better—perhaps not tomorrow, but there were dreams folded away beyond that. She must ride on the wings of such hope until she and Cole could be together, managing somehow to bring together the two separate lives they had built apart...

The thought was troubling. Only the Lord knew how much she had hoped that Cole would find a way of being with her for the holidays—how she had prayed, keeping vigil night after night, listening for an unexpected hoofbeat...which never came. Being apart as they had on the trail to Oregon served to fan the flame of their affection, making each platonic reunion something more than a maturing friendship. Each time they were together was more exciting but less satisfying than the last—until they had their *one* night of total togetherness—to have and to hold. Was the wonder of that night what the Bible meant by knowing—really *knowing*—each other? Rachel clung to the memory desperately, hoping that it was enough, all the while trying to push the dark misgivings away. But that was as futile as trying to push back the wind. Only prayer sustained her through those times.

Nearing the settlement, Rachel realized that the afternoon had slipped into near-twilight and that the air had gentled. Branches that had been dripping with rain were drying now as the clouds parted to show the winter sun. The valley wound into the hills. She saw the dark fields, now bearded with new wheat, and imagined Cole home to stay long before threshing time. Rachel slowed her horse and looked into the sky. Its patches of blue were eternal, something to depend on. The sky went on forever, helping to bring back her spiritual perspective.

Then, with her face upturned, Rachel's ears caught the unmistakable sound of hoofbeats. For one moment she dared hope. . . then her hope turned to fear. How close was she to the village? But even as she asked herself the question, she realized that it was not one horse, or two, but a countless number she heard. And, yes, the turn of wagon wheels.

Help. Help had come! The supply wagons mentioned at Thanksgiving were here at last. The wagons had made the turn leading into the village and she could hear the welcoming screams of the children. Urging Hannibal forward, she raced to catch the last of the wagons and gradually moved to the next and then the next. Cole was not among them. There was disappointment which changed to a monster of anger. And for the first time something akin to jealousy sank its fangs into her heart. These men could get through, but her husband could not. "Make me understand, Lord," she whispered, trying to compose herself as she went forth to meet the men, "why men must put work before love, making it a woman's rival."

To Rachel's surprise, General Wilkes—looking as distinguished in his military uniform as before—was among the company. Dismounting, the grayhaired gentleman bowed. Then, removing a leather glove, he extended his hand.

"Ah, my dear Mrs. Lord—as lovely as ever," he smiled gallantly. Even as Rachel thanked him softly, she was aware that the gubernatorial candidate's piercing eyes were examining her hand. "If you will pardon my saying so, my lovely lady, I note in you a strange incongruity—the delicacy of your face and form, as opposed to the work-calloused hands."

Rachel smiled, finding herself liking the polished honesty of the man. "Which qualifies me for the pioneer wife, wouldn't you say, General Wilkes?"

"That," he said wistfully, "and more. A man, such as Colby Lord is destined to be, needs the support of such a lady. I know—having lost my own dear wife—" His voice faltered a moment, but he recovered quickly. "Yes, you are as puzzling as the land in which we live. What kind of woman, pray, would receive us as graciously as you, attend the meetings obviously well-informed, and remain genteel—even while astride a stallion!"

The Lord had heard her prayers. Rachel suddenly saw herself anew and liked what she saw. That she was an ideal wife was all she asked; all the rest had been added. She favored General Wilkes with a smile. Buck joined them then. There were handshakes, and Rachel was about to move away when the general turned back to her.

"I was asked to deliver this to you, Mrs. Lord—a letter from your husband."

My dearest, beautiful Rachel, Cole's letter began. Rachel felt her knees trembling and sat down quickly in the sanctuary of the cabin, where she had come before going for Star. Now her eyes skimmed the pages hurriedly.

> It is wet and cold here—as though the sun will never shine again. But it is shining on you, dear one, as it always shines on us when we are together. Until then I walk in the sunlight of your love . . . .

Rachel read the paragraph over and over. Then she scanned the rest of the lengthy letter. Cole was busy—so busy. He had secured the necessary grants, and there were commitments from at least a dozen merchants wishing to establish themselves in the village. Steamboats would tie up as hoped there at the mouth of the river—providing they could talk the beavers out of moving their dams! Did Rachel know beavers were monogamous—like himself? (Rachel paused and smiled with tears in her eyes— *oh, wonderful Cole!*)

There was more about meetings, his search for a minister (could she help him convince Brother Davey that the new man would be his "assistant"?), and a teacher. In the interim, would she and Yolanda be willing . . .

Rachel inhaled deeply. How unfair she had been— thinking only of herself! She would have so much to write Cole!

But first to finish his letter. Cole had surprises for both her and Star . . . but then something caught her eye—a warning to be cautious—aware *always* that danger is near. Then, "Until we can be together, Sweetheart, we have God's love to lean on."

30

The Prodigal

There was a wild flurry of activity after the supplies arrived. Trees, deadened by cutting off a ring of bark, were cut down, and then corn kernels "hoed in" between them—the soil being so rich and mellow that it required no plowing. This left teams free for hauling logs down the mountainsides to be sawed into boards. Yes, there was a sawmill now, Cole having sent all the makings. There could be shakes for the roofs, timbers for the flooring, and rails split for fencing one man's kingdom apart from all others. For "out there" (meaning apart from the village) was their land—*theirs*. They had papers to make it legal now. All they need do was "prove up" on the land by living on it six months.

It was a gift from heaven—all of it. The settlers looked upon the growth around them with a kind of awe that bordered on reverence. Owning the land came nigh on to making heaven and earth one. Windows, now glassed, looked out on both.

There was only one parcel in question: Superstition Mountain! The men that Cole sent along with General Wilkes seemed to think this was important. Originally, according to the recorded deeds, Judson Lee's property line came so close that with a bit of coaxing he could have become the owner. But he had never bothered. Let the Indians bury their dead there...maybe 'twas their Happy Hunting Ground ...certainly he be of no mind to interfere. Spirits of departed souls be in no need of "meetin' in th' flesh!"

And so it had stood until Cole filed claim for the mountain as a completion to the city site. It was then that he learned, according to the general's report, that there was a prior claim under what appeared to be an assumed name, since the man could not be found. Probably a rumor about the gold...but ownership was necessary.

Why was it important? the council wondered aloud. Well, it formed a barrier—just good business to surround a city with walls. Also, the Indians belonged on the reservation, and as long as they deemed the mountain sacred, it would be a source of conflict. Already there was discontent—actually a downright threat of wiping out the white men from the valley. That explained the barrels of gunpowder.

Rachel, hearing the reports, questioned Buck anxiously.

"Are you afraid?" She asked.

"Not afraid, just cautious. And let's continue to keep Star in sight." He hesitated before continuing, and when he spoke his eyes did not meet Rachel's. "Did you know that Cole had a chance meeting with none other than Julius Doogan in Portland?"

Rachel felt her face blanch. "What did he say?"

"Julius? I don't know—but the general says the

man has had half a dozen skirmishes with the law.
You knew, didn't you?" The question seemed to
surprise Buck as much as it surprised Rachel.

She nodded. It was time for the truth.

"The man on the mountain?"

"Yes—one of them. The other things I don't know
about."

"And Yolanda's with him?" The words were the
harshest she had ever heard from this gentle man.

"I don't know, Buck. I'm afraid—"

"Don't be," he said, laying a hand on her arm. But
she heard hurt in his voice.

In the month that followed, Rachel was thankful
for the dizzying pace of activity. Hammers thudding
against wood and saws gnawing into bark brought
her a comforting sense of civilization. Temporarily
she could forget the threats of war with the Indians.
And Agnes Grant had given up her mission of
"sightings"—or else the settlers were too busy with
their own lives to pay attention to her prattling
tongue.

When the snows came, the building slowed somewhat. The families were unable to move into
individual cabins as quickly as they had hoped, so
there was not enough room to store all the grain,
staple groceries, and hardware. The men discussed
the matter following church on a late February
Sunday.

"There be no problem amongst us," Judson Lee
declared. "Us old-timers 'ave granaries 'n barns fer
housin' 'em."

It was during the moving process that Yolanda
came home. Rachel had had an especially trying day
at school. Without Aunt Em she was sure she would
never have made it. But the woman, behaving like
the spiritual mother of the multitude, took over
large groups for Bible story time, leaving Rachel a

period for working with penmanship and the conjugation of some Latin verbs with the older children.

That night, bone-tired, she had crawled gratefully into bed. She fell asleep immediately, only to be awakened by a tapping on the front door. Forgetting caution, she called out a sleepy, "Who's there?"

"It's Yolanda—oh, Rachel, please—may I come in?"

The two girls fell into each other's arms, too overcome for words. Yolanda was safe. To Rachel that was all that mattered. But for Yolanda it was not enough. In time she said in a voice still choked with tears, "Now, if we've had that 15-handkerchief cry, I have to talk—"

And talk they did. Dawn was breaking by the time it was finished. Yolanda had gone away with Julius, thinking they would be married. The man had no such intentions, Yolanda admitted in a voice much too small for her. She was ashamed—oh, so ashamed. (At that point she pressed a hand over her face convulsively and had to be comforted.)

Once Rachel got her past the terrible remorse and self-hatred that assailed her, she was able to go on with the painful story. Julius had begged her to stay with him. She had held out for marriage, only to find that she did not want marriage either. She did not want to be betrothed, have a wedding, and make a home with him. She just wanted to go on meeting him in secret...facing the opposition as a part of the exciting adventure...she just wanted—*being in love.*

Rachel held Yolanda to her as one holds a distraught child. "Oh, Yolanda, that isn't how a love story goes—" then, seeing the hurt and bewilderment in Yolanda's face, she switched tactics. "Why did he want you with him?"

Yolanda's voice was suddenly laced with anger. "Not for the reasons you would guess! It had to do with Superstition Mountain—his wanting ownership. He needed a wife for that much ground—*oh, this is so embarrassing!*—then when he found that Pa had staked a claim, he—he wanted to use me as a bargaining piece—to force Pa's hand. He thought there was gold—or pretended he did. Oh, Rachel, he never loved me—*never*—"

"Maybe he did in his way, Yolanda. Let's not be too hard on him," Rachel found herself saying. "Ours is a story of forgiveness here in the settlement. And God's Word leaves us no choice."

It was not that she would have defended the man, Rachel thought slowly. The human part of her would like nothing better than seeing him punished. But the heart of her knew that vengeance belonged solely to the Lord. And so she did not tell Yolanda of Julius Doogan's unwelcome advances and his threats when extracting a promise from her, nor did she share what might be the possible good in him—in case it *was* he who assisted in bringing little Callie into the world.

"Whoso diggeth a pit shall fall therein."

Yolanda, blowing her nose, did not hear Rachel's Proverb. "Rachel," she whispered, "can *you* forgive me—overlook our differences—?"

"What differences?" Rachel asked innocently. And together they laughed, renewing a seasoned friendship...

It was understandable that Yolanda would dread the encounter with her father. Rachel suggested that she stay and help with classes, and then they would face his wrath together.

But there was no wrath.

Judson Lee, just as it was in the Biblical account, saw them "from afar." His eager but wordless greeting said that he had watched the trail for his prodigal daughter's return every minute of every day.

He simply put out his arms. And Yolanda, her face twitching with emotion, walked into them.

Then, thrusting her almost roughly aside, the rugged giant of a man said, "Meet yer baby sister— then hustle some biscuits."

His tone said clearly that the matter would never be mentioned again in this household. *Forgiveness.* What a beautiful word!

31

Return of the Raven

Yolanda, quick to agree that work was the best medicine for a broken heart, became deeply dedicated to helping at the school. With her assistance, and generally that of Aunt Em, Rachel found her own workload reduced. More importantly, the children were learning remarkably fast considering that none of the three women were credentialed teachers.

In fact, all was going well—almost too well—in the valley. Cabins were taking shape on the freshly scarred land. The sawmill, with volunteer labor for the present, was operating throughout the daylight hours. Judson Lee had resumed his fishing and, reassured that boats would tie up soon (bringing buyers with contracts for his salted-down fish) often worked at the mill after it had closed for the day in order to turn out staves for the boys to fashion into storage barrels. Young orchards flowered. Cows pastured along the lowlands. Sheep bleated from the upper mountainsides. And housewives began setting their hens for spring chicks.

And then the rumors commenced again. The riderless horse...strange fires at night...and the raven, circling so low that one could see his talons, giving out strange warning sounds, and then swooping back to Superstition Mountain. Unease that had lain dormant in some far corner surfaced in Rachel's mind, demanding to be dealt with.

Could it be the Indians, as some claimed? Or was it, she wondered suddenly, Julius Doogan again—his warped mind trying to spook the settlers into staying away from what he so coveted? If so, where was the law? Was there not a warrant out for his arrest? Was there gold, as he claimed, or—?

Try as she would, Rachel could find no answers. As advised, she kept Star even closer to her side. Star, always unquestioningly obedient, enjoyed their closeness, often slipping a small brown hand into Rachel's to say, "I love you, Mother mine. And we love our Daddy, yes?"

That is why her sudden disappearance was such a complete shock. It was out of keeping. It was impossible.

One moment the near-translucent child was here. The next she was gone, her baby-hands taking Rachel's heart with her back into the vapor from which she had appeared on the trail.

Yolanda was sure she was with Aunt Em. But, no, Aunt Em said (not too worriedly at that point), Star was with some of the other children—drawing their pictures, no doubt. No? Then, Brother Davey...

Frantically Rachel looked for Brother Davey, alerting everyone she saw. They joined the search—calling, calling, in voices that mourned. The inevitable had happened.

Moreover. Of course, the dog would find the child.

With renewed hope, Rachel ran to the cabin where he was leashed while the children were in school. The great animal whined as if he knew something was wrong, his great body pushing Rachel aside as he scrambled to freedom. At first the dog seemed to pick up the trail. Then, with a lost look in his eyes, he returned to Rachel.

Rachel, in her dark world of grief, blamed herself. She had not watched after this special God-given child. Then without warning her guilt turned to anger—anger at Cole. What kind of husband and father would leave his family in pursuit of a dream? The strength in her bones was gone, as was her reasoning power. Her heart shriveled and then died . . .

She must have stood for hours impervious to the activity around her. She was hardly conscious of Brother Davey's whizzing past demanding that he be told what was going on. "Everybody jest come chargin' past me like a herd o' buffalo—tellin' me nothin'!"

And then Buck was at her side. "Drink this!" he commanded, forcing a mug of scalding coffee into her hand, then pushing her hand to her mouth. "Drink it and brace up—there's a job ahead. We have to widen the search. She isn't in the village—"

Star isn't in the village. If Cole had been here, I would not have lost my child. Like a war drum the words beat in her head as she watched the grim-faced men equip themselves to extend the search. They would tramp out the woods, they said. And Yolanda would hurry home, just in case Star could have taken a notion to see Callie again. Woodenly Rachel listened, knowing in her heart that the search was futile.

The sun lowered and the men lighted lanterns against the dark. Could she have wandered up the mountain? The child had such a curious mind, they said. Perhaps she was fascinated by stories...

Superstition Mountain. "I don't think so," Rachel said. And, yet, even as she spoke, there was a terrible shortness of breath and an ache where her heart used to be.

It was Buck who told her they were going to search the mine. "It's just a precaution—nobody believes she would have wandered up there."

Rachel turned tortured eyes to his, watching the wind ruffle his hair. How tired he looked! Maybe he and Yolanda would have a chance at happiness now—more of a chance than she herself had had. She must remember to give Yolanda the little patch of yellow as a talisman...

"Rachel, are you all right? Everybody is going up the mountain. I want you to come, just in case—"

Rachel, unable to speak, shook her head. She must stay here. Estrellita, her Little Star, might reappear...

All night the dragging sound went on. The men had taken chains, a rope ladder, and a great shovel for lowering into the old mine. Lanterns formed a weird circle of light around the mountain peak, and it was easy to imagine the great raven circling above, his black eyes evil and mocking.

Sleep would not come. Without lighting a lamp, Rachel sat dry-eyed by the window watching... watching...watching...until at last she drifted into a sort of hypnotic stupor, hoping—although unable to ask it of the Lord—that she would never awaken.

When there was a tapping at the door, it seemed a natural part of the midnight madness that Poe's raven should come to pick the dry bones of her grief. Rachel...*Rachel!*

But she did not answer—not even after the door creaked open and the voice called out to her in the inside darkness of the room.

The shadowy figure came close. She rose and stepped forward. Why keep fate waiting? The shadow caught her in its arms and held her a prisoner. For a moment she did not struggle. And then the stupor lifted and Rachel was wide awake. She was in the arms of her husband...beating his chest in fury.

"Why weren't you here when we needed you? Why have you come *now*?" she cried out, anger her master. And she struggled, but it was no use. She was no match for Colby Lord. She never had been. Not in love...or war...or...

"I'm here because I love you." Cole was shaking her gently. "I'm here because I love Star—"

"You know?" Her voice, like her heart, was dead.

"I saw the lights—heard the noise—and felt the time had come to investigate the strange reports. Then when I found out the truth, my next thought was of you. Oh, Rachel, this is a time when we need each other—"

"There have been many such times."

Cole winced. Then his arms tightened, and when he spoke there was wretchedness in his voice. "I know, my darling. I know I have failed you. If I could go back, I would make no such sacrifices."

"We can't go back, Cole. We can never go back."

"I will make it all up to you—you and Star. We will find her, darling Rachel. We *have* to—and now we must go!"

Daylight was streaking through the window. Cole was already fumbling in the half-light to find her coat...a scarf...

"I'm not going with you!"

"Oh, yes, you are!" Without warning he bundled her lifeless body into a cape and, in what seemed like one unbroken movement, lifted her up, carried her out, and swung her onto the back of his waiting horse.

Again the unreality. The heartbreak mixed with madness. And a million questions left unanswered. But, even in the face of tragedy, Rachel was aware of the familiar strength of Cole's chest as she leaned against him—the wind lifting her hair and her skirts—and her desperate need of him. She wanted to tell him. But the wind sucked her breath away. And then it was too late.

32

The Silent Scream

All night there had been a cold drizzle. On top of the mountain the drizzle had turned to fog which draped itself around the peak like an ill-fitting shroud.

Rachel had not wanted to come. But once there, she joined with the others with a sense of calm that surprised her. Was there any sign? *No.* Was the dragging of the mine complete? *Yes, nothing there—no recent, uh, skeletons—just fossils, undoubtedly Indian.* No evidence then of foul play? *No, but there had to be unless—wild animals—*

It was Moreover who found her. The dog nosed his way immediately into the bushes, pushing past boulders, and whining. Rachel followed, fighting down the panic inside. That the dog would find the vapor child there was no doubt. But would she be alive? *Wild animals!* Rachel shuddered.

When the dog stopped, Rachel pushed through the

181

undergrowth of manzanita and laurel, laced with ropes of blackberry vines. All of them tore at her skin as if to guard their prisoner. But Rachel was impervious to the pain of scratches, her eyes blinded to the sight of the blood which trickled down her arms.

Star, her elfin body curled into an egg-shape, sat beneath an obviously man-made shelter of fir boughs, her great eyes searching Rachel's with a maturity beyond her years. It was Rachel who burst into hysterical sobs.

The child clung to her, whispering words of comfort. "It's all right, Mother mine. It is as he told me. 'Wait,' he said, 'and there will be no danger for you and your familia, su madre, su padre, y sus amigos.' Comprehende?" Excited now, Star had reverted back to her native tongue.

"Who, Darling, *who*?" Rachel whispered as she wrapped the child in her woolen cape. "And, yes, I understand."

Star snuggled close to her breast. "The man in the picture," she said.

The man in the picture. A quick rollback of memory brought Rachel face to face with Julius Doogan, whose picture Star had sketched. Why would he steal Star away—then protect her?

Together they were stumbling through the brush and Rachel was calling frantically, "Cole, *Cole*..." and all the while her mind was asking: Why, *why*, WHY?

Rachel felt herself growing dizzy from the shock of it all. The sense of weakness she had been experiencing was back. *Oh, dear Lord, hold me up a little longer*, she willed.

Then she saw Cole's face. Grave with concern, it came closer. Great waves of relief swept over her as Cole wound his arms around them both.

"Julius—Julius Doogan," she gasped.

"Dad-*dee*!" The word was a little squeal of delight from Star. "The man saved me from the Indians. I was to wait for you. Then God came and brought you. He heard me, Daddy."

33

Raid!

Too exhausted physically and emotionally to attempt conversation, Rachel tried to fit together the crazy puzzle as Cole led the way back. The others would have questions. And how could she answer when there were so many pieces missing? Almost— *almost*—parts of it would make sense. Then her vision would blur again, and nothing made sense at all. Some day perhaps she, Cole, Buck, and Star could piece it all into a logical pattern.

For now it took all her energy to keep her footing on the slippery trail. Star, wound in the cocoon of Rachel's cape and cradled in Cole's arms, was still chatting away about the Indians. Rachel could only surmise that Julius Doogan, being of a strangely dual personality, had been unable to live with the story he had told the Indians about Star's being of their blood. But, to save his own scalp, the man had deemed it wiser to remove the child than to right the mistruth . . . but for how long? And why?

Rachel could hear excited voices. Cole should be calling out the good news of Star's safety. But instead he was holding up his hand for silence.

And then Rachel heard the screams—the blood-curdling screams that told the horrible story. The cluster of cabins which were home to so many, the village which was the beginning of Cole's dream, was under attack. The Indians *had* come.

"Quiet—we must be very quiet," Buck was saying as calmly as if he were announcing a meeting for the council.

But his warnings were of no avail to the hysterical Agnes Grant. "Th' rim of fire! I told you it was coming—only it's down there now 'stead of up here! A repeat of Sodom 'n Gomorrah...maybe th' end of time!"

"Shut up, Aggie!" Aunt Em had walked to stand beside the screaming woman. "If there's blood shed, it'll be partly on your hands—talkin' th' ears off'n an acre o' corn th' way you do! One more word 'n I'll gag you!"

Now the screams below were mingled with the sound of exploding gunfire. *Guns? The Indians had guns?* As the questions churned in her mind, Rachel—using her last measure of energy—lifted her eyes to the fiery scene below. Then, just as there was the sound of a bugle call—a *bugle?*—she collapsed at the feet of her husband. She felt the cold sting of rain.

Some distant part of her wanted to say, "I'm sorry." But there were no voices in the netherworld into which she had drifted. Neither did there seem to be a path that led back.

34

To Dream Anew

Waking in the darkness, Rachel—drowsy with half-sleep and a strange inertia—thought she was in the little cabin she once called home. Then consciousness stirred. She must be out-of-doors. A canopy of stars glistened overhead and a thin last-phase moon was rising in the east. But the rain! What had happened to the rain?

Rachel felt again her terror of looking down on the burning village under a ceiling of crimson clouds, knowing that somewhere in all that glowing cinder that had once been a haven for Oregon's newest settlers a dream was dying. Cole's.

She tried to move, but her limbs felt heavy. A day had gone out of her life. How did one recapture it? Maybe if she could remember, she would understand why Julius led them away—

The fire...and then what? The explosion of gunfire...the crazed shouting...and then the bugle. The Cavalry—the Cavalry had come! They would have quelled the uprising...but the fire? And then she remembered. The windows of the sky had opened up, as if God had come to their aid, and the rain had come down in torrents...

Then the face of Aunt Em, faint and distorted, then coming into focus, leaned over her. There was concern in her voice.

"You've slept a spell, Dearie—hit your head in that nasty fall. Don't try 'n talk. We're all right. No killin' and Aggie's repented! Cavalry took th' Indians back to th' reservation. Th' posse—now, now, don't look so stricken—they've disbanded. Can you believe Julius Doogan's surrenderin' without no trouble? Star 'n her new China doll her daddy brought have gone with Buck 'n Yolanda t'get some supplies stored with Judson. Cole, the darlin', ordered you a poster bed with a real canopy." Aunt Em's voice drifted off dreamily, "It's gonna look mighty purty spread with that double weddin' ring quilt Nola's quiltin'...."

"Cole," Rachel whispered through dry lips. "I must go—"

"I know, but drink this herbal tea first!"

Scowling, Rachel downed the potion. There was so much to tell Cole—sometime. So much to build on here, most of the supplies having been stored elsewhere, including the gunpowder. What a blessing that the ammunition, brought in to protect them but which would have destroyed them had the fire reached the barrels, was miles away! The seed was safe...the farm machinery stored...and, most of all, the settlers and their families were alive. Maybe nobody would ever know the entire story. And did it really matter? The last few hours had taught Rachel how small, how trivial, her other concerns had been. If only Cole could forgive her...well, the Lord would give her a hand....

Rising on one elbow, she saw that only the roofs had suffered major damage. The smoke had cleared. Soon it would be safe to repair and move back. One building was not damaged: The cross rose to meet the dawn.

The door was open. Rachel's heart told her Cole would be inside.

She entered the church, walked to the altar, and—clasping her hands before her—prayed, eyes closed in silent meditation. She did not know just when Cole came to kneel beside her. But suddenly he was there, reaching out to join hands with her, reaching and then clinging.

After a while they rose to leave. But still they stood, as if this were hallowed ground, necessary to complete this delicate moment.

"It's gone," Cole whispered brokenly—"tomorrow's dream."

The despair in his voice reached out to her, causing sudden tears to gather and the heart she had thought dead to quicken. Cole needed her as never before. She *was* at his table!

"Dreams are never gone, Cole," Rachel said softly. "They only shift positions."

"We can never go back. It is true what you said."

"But we can go forward. I expected too much, Cole—demanded too much. Yet I feared to be open. Oh, please forgive me!"

"Open? How could you be? I was not here for you. It is I who begs forgiveness, yours and the Lord's. I attempted the impossible—"

"But He did the impossible for us, my darling!" Rachel sang out, unable to keep her secret any longer. "And now I expect you to go on with your dream for me, for Star—and for your son!"

Cole lifted his head. "Son," he whispered. "A *child*?"

In one forward motion Cole pulled her to him. Then he lifted her in the cradle of his arms with gentle tenderness.

"A child," he whispered again, as if repeating the words would make him believe the miracle.

Rachel nodded against his chest.

Neither of them spoke further. No words could express the *knowing*. Their yesterdays were gone. And today no longer mattered. The corners of all their dreams came together in a beautiful patchwork design. The larger dream they shared reached beyond tomorrow—into the Eternity that God has prepared for those who truly love.